AN UNEXPECTED VISIT

Joseph Falank

Winter Goose
PUBLISHING
where words take flight

Winter Goose Publishing
45 Lafayette Road #114
North Hampton, NH 03862

www.wintergoosepublishing.com
Contact Information: info@wintergoosepublishing.com

An Unexpected Visit

COPYRIGHT © 2016 by Joseph Falank

First Edition, October 2016

Cover Design by Joseph Falank
Typesetting by Odyssey Books

ISBN: 978-1-941058-54-1

Published in the United States of America

For my wife, Becca, who forever supports the dream
For my daughter, who looks at me like I can do no wrong
For Jessica Kristie, who published my first, second, and now third book,
and continues to leave the door open

"One of the keys to happiness is a bad memory."
—Rita Mae Brown

"I'm not perfect. Remember that,
and try to forgive me when I fail you."
—Elizabeth Lowell, *Sweet Wind, Wild Wind*

OVERTURE

Before I get into it, I want to share with you the disclaimer that the experience scrawled out in the following pages took place a long time ago. I was twelve at the time. A child. Unlike today's youth who have unlimited access to the world via smartphones and their own Facebook pages, who also wield the dangerous and terrifying ability to sext obscene photographs to each other, I grew up distracted by much more . . . innocent things, things like after-school cartoons, videogames that weren't about ultra-violence, playing Manhunt in the woods, and Magic the Gathering. Yes, I was a nerd. However, given my age at the time of the long weekend spent with my estranged father, know that what I am about to tell you is not—I repeat and emphasize *is not*—a story for children. It really isn't a story at all. The word *story* carries a misleading connotation that implies *fiction*. The purpose of documenting it here is an attempt—a desperate one—to use my God-given talent to write as a way to confront the past, and, hopefully, once it's all out on the page, be done with it. My therapist thinks it's a wonderful idea. I pay good money for her opinions.

I also want to preface that while I am in my mid-thirties now (and a writer . . . again, don't get that confused with storyteller—I scribe sports and leisure columns for the local Serling Oaks Times), and where you may believe that the long, winding road of time has hazed my recollection of the events, let me cast assurance that while my memory isn't as sharp as a fresh number two pencil (my wife and the exact date of our anniversary can testify to that), when it comes to the visit with my father in the dead of winter 1995, there are just some things in life that refuse to be forgotten.

Memory's a bitch that way.

I remember it all. From sights and sounds to even smells and the dialogue we shared, but especially how it felt that second night when he had me by the throat with both of his wiry, calloused hands . . . It's all clutter I've never been able to fully clear out of the ol' headspace.

Perhaps the most important note I want to make clear before I begin is that I cannot control readers' opinions, and, with that said, want to stress that this portrayal of events is not meant to eviscerate nor dishonor the character of my father. My father served his country proudly given the unique tasks he was called upon for. I suppose that was *his* God-given talent. This is also not a criticism or a diatribe against military life—how it can coarsely affect a family, or take its toll on one's psyche. I believe those facets have been better documented elsewhere, and with far greater focus on the details and facts than I will be presenting here. My hope, if you take anything away from my experience, is a growing awareness for another human being's suffering when they aren't showing visible signs, plus also the comfort in knowing I, Noah Adams, survived to tell the tale (again, not fiction, but couldn't escape the catchiness of the wording). In that knowledge, though, realize that sometimes there are far greater costs than paying with your life.

I want to apologize if the following disturbs you in any way. That's not the purpose, however everything has its unintended side effects. The sun can brighten a beautiful summer day and do wonders for the plant and animal life, not to mention give us reason to sit out on our back decks at dusk, taking in the wonders of a sunset with a drink by our side.

The sun, lest we forget, can also burn.

TUESDAY

It was in the middle of a frigid February afternoon that I learned I would be spending the coming three-day weekend with my father. The last bell of the day at East Serling Oaks Middle School chimed at two thirty; I bolted out of math class in a blaze of excitement. The glee in my racing steps to my locker to collect my coat and gloves had nothing to do with getting home quick to start my homework, and instead everything to do with the daily snowball skirmishes my friends and I had on our trek home. There was still good snow on the ground that day for the purposes of snowball making, though it'd been sitting around awhile and become a little on the grimy side. Looking back, there was nary a sign to warn me that something bad was looming on the horizon. Unless you count that I took a wayward snowball smack in the nose from my friend Jerry about a block away from the school. While in a daze from the shot, and my glove off to check for any bleeding, my retaliatory throw came out of a pile of fresh yellow snow I'd unknowingly jammed my naked hand into. If that counts for anything, then I had two strikes against me by the time I reached home.

Nevertheless, upon entering through the backdoor into the kitchen, I noticed an intense change in the atmosphere. This was different from other days when I'd come inside to the intoxicating aroma of freshly made hot chocolate Mom would prepare and have waiting for me on the stove. But that Tuesday there was no steaming mug sitting between the burners. And I don't know how else to describe what my senses picked up on when entering the house other than the air had been still. Dense. Hostile.

"Hey Mom," I said, then closed the door behind me. She didn't answer. Strange. "Mom?"

I swiped the bottoms of my boots across the interior floor mat several times to remove the remnant mush of snow stuck to the treads. Mom would have strung me outside by my toes if I'd walked through the house sloshing footsteps of melted snow along the way. If my mother had a pet peeve it was stepping in someone else's wet tracks while she was clad in her socks. She also disliked drivers who incessantly hit their brakes for no reason. And Publisher's Clearing House. She thought that whole thing about people showing up at your door with a huge check was complete horseshit.

"Mom?" I called a third time. One boot I managed to fling off and into the pantry. The second one was giving me problems because it's always too much trouble for a twelve-year-old boy to bend down and undo the Velcro straps by hand. Just work it off using the opposite foot and toss it. It took a little finagling before I managed the second boot off and flailed it into the pantry along with the other. It was then I heard my mother's voice, but it wasn't in response to me.

"Yeah, Ginny, that's what he said."

Ginny—Aunt Ginny—was my mom's sister, who lived out in Akron, Ohio. Mom was on the phone with her. In socked feet I quietly slid across the linoleum floor, stopping short of the archway between the kitchen and dining room where I listened in, my back pressed up against the side of the refrigerator, its humming giving off a slight vibration against my spine.

"I don't know what's gotten into him," Mom said.

My ears perked at the tone of her distress. It hit me much like Jerry's snowball had—hard and cold—except this wasn't a strike to the face as much as it was an uneasy quiver through the knot of my guts. My Spidey-senses picked up trouble.

"He hasn't called in forever," my mother went on saying. "He hasn't done a damned thing for us. Not a goddamn thing. But now, all of a sudden, he's demanding to see his son."

I swallowed but there wasn't an ounce of saliva in my throat. My mouth had gone bone dry at the mention of my father. I laid the back of my head to rest against the side of the fridge, continuing to eavesdrop.

"Yeah, that's what he said; he wants Noah for the weekend."

My eyes squeezed shut. Angst brought on a tightening ache across my belly. I tried swallowing again but my mouth was still as parched as the middle of the sun-scorched Mojave. Bluntly, I knew I was fucked. Capital F.

There was a brief pause on my mother's side of the conversation. From my hiding spot just behind the doorway in the kitchen I could barely make out the agitated mumblings of my aunt through the phone. No doubt she was cursing my father as well—cursing every hair follicle, every drop of blood, every little genome that made up his very existence.

"Exactly, Ginny," my mother said. "He hasn't helped pay one god-damn bill around this house, not even so much as made a phone call. Hasn't even sent a fucking birthday card to his own son. Nothing in two years, not since we found out he was back and didn't tell us. And now he has the gall to demand this of me."

Hearing my mother drop the F-word was actually kind of intimidating. She hardly ever used language like that around me, even when she was beyond pissed and the words could be seen written across her face. Like when I brought home a failing grade on a Social Studies test a few months earlier. I had neglected to study. She substituted her choice of words, but I wasn't fooled. I knew what was brewing beneath the surface. And even though my mother didn't know I was just around the corner listening in when she let her angry words fly, it was startling to witness and hear the depths of anger she was capable of.

"I know he has no grounds," Mom said to Aunt Ginny. "He has no ground to stand on to be making such threats. But I'm doing it, Ginny." She sounded worn down. Defeated. The anger subsided from her voice. "Noah deserves to have some sort of relationship with his father, if Scott's willing to try."

I sighed, closed my eyes, defeated. Capital F.

"Noah's twelve. He doesn't need to know what kind of asshole his father is at this age. He'll figure it out when he's older."

Ginny began rambling on in response as I sunk into a seated position against the fridge. Two things were going on inside me at that moment: The first was bitter disgust. I didn't want to hear any more bad-talk about my father, especially seeing as a visit with him was now imminent. The second thing I felt was guilt for eavesdropping. It would do no good for my mother to turn around in her chair and notice I had heard everything that dropped out of her mouth for the last three minutes. My father had been laid out across a sacrificial table between her and my aunt and flayed like a trout. Their words were ugly, repulsive. And I feared they were true. Was he really threatening my mother when it came to seeing me? And why, out of the blue, did he want to see me *now*?

At the time of Mom and Ginny's conversation, I didn't have much in the way of strong feelings toward my father. When I was younger and he was deployed (or "activated" was the term), I remember being disappointed whenever he left, because when he wasn't somewhere in the world doing whatever he'd been called upon to do, he was home with us, and our entire relationship was different—it actually existed. My father worked for a branch of Special Forces where they spoke a lot of jargon that didn't make a lick of sense to the common man. Everything was submerged in code names and classified material. His missions weren't something he discussed openly, just telling me and Mom that he was leaving for a couple of days, or weeks, at a time, and that he'd be right back. He always came back. And of course I was elated to have him home. Aside from those my age at school, my father was my best friend. He taught me how to fish, how to properly throw a fastball, and the uncanny ability to fart on command (hint: you have to kneel a certain way for air to enter your backside and fill your tummy. You're welcome.).

The last . . . activation . . . was different, though. My father did eventually return from whatever mission he was sent on, but for reasons unknown to me and Mom, it wasn't us he came back to.

He'd bought an old farmhouse out in the sticks of Dalton in the vast

Pennsylvania countryside, about an hour south of where we lived in Serling Oaks, New York. My father had come back from his assignment and never told us. My mother discovered his return when a friend who lived in PA happened to notice his name listed under housing transactions. Mom didn't know what it meant. Was their marriage over? Had he left us for someone else? A whole other family altogether? She also had no way of contacting him. Once or twice, I believe, she considered driving down to this house and confronting him, but reasoned that if he hadn't tried making contact then he probably didn't want anything to do with us.

Then, one day, weeks after my mother and I learned of his new residence in PA, the telephone rang. There was no Caller ID back then, but I knew it was him. Call it a sixth sense.

The conversation—only privy to me because I picked up the upstairs phone the exact moment my mother did downstairs—went a little something like this:

MOM: Hello?

A long pause.

MOM: Hello?

HIM: (Quietly) Maggie . . .

MOM: *Scott?* Scott . . . what the hell is—

HIM: I can't explain everything right now, okay? I just want you to know I'm all right.

MOM: Scott . . . why didn't you come home? What's this about you buying a house in Pennsylvania?

HIM: . . .

MOM: Scott? You say you're all right but you're obviously not all right—

HIM: (His voice carries through soft weeping) I'm sorry. I'm sorry. I couldn't do it.

MOM: You're sorry? Couldn't do what, Scott?

HIM: I can't look at you. Or you me.

MOM: What? Scott, you're not making any sense . . .

HIM: It has to be this way. It *has* to. For now.

MOM: Scott, listen to me . . .

HIM: I wish I could be better but—

MOM: *Scott!*

HIM: . . .

MOM: (Now also sobbing) Scott . . . Scott, you have to think about your son—*our* son. Noah. Noah's here, he's upstairs playing in his room—he's been waiting for you, Scott. You always come back to him. He's only ten for Christ sakes, he doesn't understand any of this. I don't know what happened after you left but you need to come back . . . for your son . . .

HIM: You have to do it. You have to tell him I can't. I can't see him. Not right now.

MOM: (Crying) . . . why? (Sniffles, gains composure) Tell me what happened, Scott.

HIM: Tell him I love him, but tell him I can't have him around right now. I can't see him—

MOM: We can fix this. Whatever is happening we can fix it.

HIM: —maybe someday—

MOM: We can all be together again.

HIM: Can you do that, Maggie? Can you tell him?

A long pause.

HIM: Maggie?

MOM: No, Scott. I won't tell him.

HIM: Why?

MOM: . . .

HIM: Maggie?

MOM: Because you already did.

HIM: What?

MOM: Noah. He's listening in on the upstairs phone.

No one uttered a word as I hung up.

Very quickly my mind—my ten-year-old mind—processed everything I had heard and the result was the shedding of a single tear, a tear that carried all the bundled up pain and highly-strung emotions of that moment sliding away along with it.

Two years later, standing in the kitchen, listening to the conversation between Mom and Aunt Ginny in the dining room, I didn't have much of an emotional response to seeing him again. I had moved on, learning how to exist in the world without him. Frankly, I was more disappointed the visit was going to interrupt my long weekend of hanging out with my friends and playing videogames.

I didn't want Mom to discover I'd been listening so I made a quiet retreat back across the linoleum to the backdoor. I opened and shut it again, louder this time, and called out, louder than before, that I was home. Mom was already hanging up with Aunt Ginny by the time I stepped in to see her at the dining room table.

"No hot chocolate today?" I asked, making sure to sound disappointed. Wasn't too hard.

My mother wore a frown. "I'm sorry, honey," she said. "I got caught up talking with Aunt Ginny. Time kinda got away from me. I'll make you some in just a minute. Extra marshmallows." She then bit hard on her bottom lip. "First, though, could you sit down? There's something I have to tell you."

"Is Aunt Ginny all right?" I may have overplayed the amount of concern here, but it worked to show her I had no idea what was coming.

"Oh, yeah, honey, Ginny's fine."

I hadn't noticed it much before, but my mother was a beautiful woman. Age did well for her. She had this spirally golden blond hair that never had to be dyed and was always pulled back in a bun or pony. A stray curl hung free from the hive and slinked down along her cheek, giving a garnish to her soft jawline. A very secretarial look, complimented by her horn-rimmed glasses. Beneath the lenses, her eyes were an intense green. Her pale skin flawless. But, along with really noting my mother's beauty, I also noticed that the conversation with her sister in Akron, and more likely the one that had preceded it with my father, had taken its toll, revealing every deep nook and cranny and discoloration under those eyes that her makeup had worked to conceal. What I saw in her face upon stepping past the archway into the dining room when she spun in her chair to greet me was that of a woman beaten down. Drained. Even in her defeat though, she must have put up one hell of a fight.

Still acting aloof, I dragged a chair out from the table and sat facing her, my coat still on. I let my backpack fall at my socked feet between us.

"I got a call today," she said. Her eyes lowered. She took a preparatory breath at this point before revealing the genesis of her bad news. "It was your father."

I acted confused, surprised, speechless, just as she would expect. I did feel a measure of this on the inside, and was also still reeling from what I hadn't been told yet regarding my weekend plans. Had my little performance been on a movie set, I surely would have nabbed an Oscar nom. Up yours, Tom Hanks.

Mom hesitated. Maybe she was counting on me to ask about him, wondering why I hadn't started questioning about where he'd been or why he hadn't stopped by or what he had called about. And, seriously, no goddamn birthday cards? But no such inquiry formed at my lips. After a prolonged silence from me, she said: "He . . . asked me . . . to see you this weekend."

After everything he'd done, she still covered for him. Still trying to preserve some link between him and me.

Following that phone call I had listened in on years before when my father said he wasn't coming home, Mom came up to my room and tried talking to me about the choices he had made. She defended him, saying there had to be good reason for what he had done and was continuing to do. I refused to say anything in return, just combed through my basket of action figures, improvising scenarios for them to fight while she droned on through endless sobs and sniffles trying to convince me, but more herself, that our little family wasn't broken. In the following period of time, I pretended the man didn't exist. I wouldn't talk about him. The first year was rough because he was always at the back of my thoughts. In the second year things got easier because I expected nothing and wasn't let down. I also stopped thinking about him entirely.

The first words from my mouth that acknowledged his existence in two years came during that dining room conversation. Mom mentioned him wanting to see me and, in return, I said: "What did you tell him?"

I already knew, of course. On the plus, I no longer had to hide my disappointment. Some of that disappointment was directed at her, and mostly through a look. Being deeply pissed, I hadn't had the precise words on deck in my repertoire to adequately do the situation justice.

"This sucks," said my friend Jerry. Yeah, that about summed it up. That was the word I was looking for. *Sucks* had just the right amount of pizazz.

Jerry and I had planned to meet up after checking in with our respective mothers once we'd gotten home from school. He told me to come get him at the small playground between my house and his apartment in the brick complex that was The Cove two blocks over. I found him hanging off the monkey bars of the old wooden jungle gym. He was the only one there. His discarded, and very holey gloves lay on the frozen patch of ground beneath his dangling feet. The park, which stretched the length of the street between our homes, looked like a winter wasteland with all its brown grass and neglected equipment caked over with old snow. One particular swing of the three installed was missing a chain, hanging low on its side and swaying with a rusted creak in the chilly breeze. The nets on the basketball rims had long been worn out and most of the lines severed, if not missing altogether. The blacktop of the courts was cracked and crumbling from the numerous overnight freeze overs. The wooden hull of the playground featured a few icicles and piles of hardened snow on every level but otherwise looked no worse for wear. These were the old playgrounds where it wasn't uncommon to come home with a couple of splinters embedded in your palms. Back then such a thing was a childhood rite of passage. Tetanus be damned.

Jerry huffed. "I thought we were gonna play Genesis all weekend. We were gonna try to get past the IceCap Zone together."

For all you youngins, the Genesis he referred to was a videogame system created by the company SEGA. It was popular in the early Nineties. Games came on black slabs of 16-bit cartridges and you played using wired controllers. Stone Age type stuff. I had just gotten my copy of Sonic 3 for Christmas and promised Jerry I wouldn't start without him. Obviously I didn't keep to that promise; this game was one of the very few things I specifically asked for that year, but Jerry didn't need to know otherwise. Our friendship was new so I didn't feel too bad about lying to him. Jerry had just started school at East Serling Oaks before Thanksgiving. We bonded over our mutual admiration for SEGA's mascot Sonic the Hedgehog. Jerry was still working his way through the second game in the series whenever he was over at the house, and that happened to be quite frequently. My guess was he was trying to escape the situation at his own house. Hardly did we ever spend time over there. His mom didn't make enough money for him to have a videogame system of his own, but somehow scrounged up enough to have her carton of smokes stocked in the shelves of the fridge along with a fresh box of White Zin. Jerry's father also happened to be MIA—another bonding point for us—though his father wasn't part of some elite Special Forces team. Jerry's dad had been a janitor.

The absence of a male role model in Jerry's life revealed itself in the form of some wayward behaviors. For one, Jerry tended to cut class a lot. I was never surprised to find him hanging out in the last stall of the first floor bathroom reciting the lyrics to Snoop Dogg's latest track while sketching obscene doodles on the wall in black Sharpie during fifth period Home Economics, unless we were cooking something. He was all about warm, fresh food, and managed to scarf down more than his fair share. Jerry also demonstrated a knack for snatching things, small things usually. Mostly things I couldn't conceive he would have any use for. Sometimes it was a game piece, like the top hat from the Monopoly board game. Sometimes my mother mentioned she couldn't find things like her cherry lip balm, or a loose button from one of her coats had come up missing. Aubrey, a mutual friend at school, was once reduced to tears because the New Kids on the Block magnet from the inside of her locker was gone. At the time I didn't understand, nor did I call him out on it, but in hindsight it seems Jerry's knack for being a klepto was about looking to gain some aspect of control over a much shambled home life. That being said, I knew enough back then to never show Jerry my Game Gear. It was the portable hand-held version of the Genesis machine I had gotten for my last birthday. I had Sonic games for that, too. Whenever Jerry was over, I stuck the Game Gear in the top drawer of my dresser where my underwear was. Figured it was a safe bet he wouldn't want to go digging around in there.

"Maybe you can come over next weekend and we'll play," I said. My mind wasn't really on videogames at the moment.

"When was the last time you saw him—your dad?" Jerry was beginning to grunt and strain, small bursts of steam exiting his mouth as he held the whole of his weight from the metal bars, his boots swaying as he fought to keep grip a few feet over the matted woodchips.

I didn't have to think hard about his question. Even though I spoke rarely of my father, the memories of him weren't gone entirely if I went digging for them. Like I said in the prelude: There are just some things in life that refuse to be forgotten.

"I was ten. It was right before school started up. He got a phone call in his office—he had this special phone just for work. Whenever it rang it meant he was leaving. He couldn't tell us where he was going. The day he left he did the same thing he always did."

"What?" Jerry asked, straining, but maintaining his weight.

I looked off toward the direction of the winter sun, sitting low in the westward sky. It wasn't a particularly strong sun that day. The haze of clouds obstructed enough that I didn't have to squint through the gray and onset hue of purple haze to see it. "He ruffled my hair and told me, 'You're the man now. Watch your mom for me.'"

My parents always played cautious and protected me from the specifics of my father's work, especially the worst of the news. While growing up I didn't know much about what he did, or even his rank. I only knew that he served. Even now much of his career in the Special Forces resides in the shadows. His name doesn't show up using Google searches. Mom never claimed to know much either, whether that's true or not I don't know. If she did know more than she ever said, well, kudos to her. She took that secret to her grave.

The only things I would ever really learn about him and his work were the things he told me during that long weekend.

"You remember what he looks like?" Jerry asked.

There had been pictures featuring all combinations of the three of us around the house when I was growing up. Slowly, though, like my hairline over the years, they began receding. When the whole thing went down regarding the dual discovery that not only had my father been stateside (safe and alive) without Mom and me knowing, but that he was living fifty-six miles south in an old farmhouse he purchased, all but a few of the family photographs were buried away. My mother kept one in the drawer of her nightstand next to her bed. I happened to see it one Saturday morning when I went in to wake her. The drawer was open, so I peeked inside. Underneath a dusty glass in a black frame was a picture taken in their room in the maternity ward. Mom, looking exhausted, was holding a swaddled newborn me while Dad, who looked equally exhausted, had arms around both of us. This was the first picture of the three of us after my birth.

A few months after that find, I stumbled across the rest of the pictures. We had an old laundry chute in the house that we didn't use. During an instance of dueling with some of my Batman action figures one rainy spring afternoon, I sent the Joker through the hinged door in the upstairs closet and down the easy access to the basement. When I got down to the basement, I found more than the Clown Prince of Crime inside the basket underneath the opening of the chute.

Back when I knew him, my father wore a neatly-kept beard. He had bright blue eyes—a trait other family always said I had gotten from him, that is before he chose to stay away, then they just stopped bringing it up altogether (I swear some cursed under their breath when noticing other traits he had passed along)—and a modest smile that never showed his teeth. The pictures from around the house, along with the old memory books stockpiled haphazardly in the laundry basket, wouldn't let me forget his face.

But I told Jerry I didn't really remember much. It was easier that way.

"Least your dad's a war hero," Jerry quipped. He then grunted loud as his hands slipped free of the bar. He landed on his feet with a *thunk* in the soggy woodchips. "My mom just says my dad liked the whores too much."

I had nothing to say about that.

"Hey," said Jerry in the manner of being overcome by a brilliant notion—one that thankfully changed the topic, "what if I come over tonight for dinner? After we eat we can play some Sonic for a bit."

This was yet another of Jerry's strange behavioral ticks: he had no qualms about inviting himself places when he knew there was a better deal to score elsewhere than his own home. I felt great stabs of sympathy for him a lot of the time. His mother wasn't even a novice cook by any stretch of the imagination. In fact, it was the imagination that was her problem. Jerry's dinner that night was likely to be warmed up leftover Mac & Cheese topped with going-stale Fritos again. Or a warmed up mystery casserole of some kind. Her mystery meals tended to have more combinations of day-old leftovers than the chili at Wendy's.

"Yeah," I said, in a moment of pity. "Let's go ask my mom."

We ventured through the dirty snow back to my house.

"Sorry again that I got you in the face with a snowball," Jerry said.

"That's all right," I said. "Sorry I threw a pee ball at you."

He forgave me.

"Sucks again that you have to spend the weekend with your dad."

"Yeah," I said. It did.

When we got to my house, I ran upstairs ahead of him and stashed my Game Gear deep in my top drawer, among many pairs of underwear.

THURSDAY

At around eight fifteen on the night before the visit with my father, the telephone rang. I was sitting on the floor of my bedroom cross-legged, hunched toward the gigantic hand-me-down floor model television set, videogame controller in my sweaty grasp. Mom had just finished laying out fresh laundry on the bed for me to fold and put away. We both paused. As the four-tone background track of the game continued to play backdrop to the second and third rings of the phone carrying throughout the house, she turned to look at me. It is my belief now that at least once in a person's life they will experience the same unexplainable phenomenon as I had in that moment. When you know something you have no business knowing, and, as a bonus to that, you share this experience with someone in the same vicinity as you. Of course it's never anything truly worthwhile, like lotto numbers, or the answer to Final Jeopardy.

Without a word between us, by the look on my mother's face, I knew we were thinking the same thing. It was my father calling.

There was a corded phone out on a small stand in the hall. My mother, standing at the cusp of my doorway, shifted the empty laundry basket under one arm, and reached out to answer it. I could see the hesitation in her action, and hear it in the softness of her voice when the speaker end was up to her mouth.

"Hello?"

She listened for a moment, eyes narrowing. I leaned further forward, having to scoot about a foot closer to the television on the thin burgundy carpet, to reach the knob and lower the volume. Only thing I could make out was a low, indecipherable tone from the other end of the line.

"It's late, Scott," my mother said with a sigh in her voice. She set the basket down at her feet and rubbed at the creases that appeared on her forehead with her newly freed hand as if chasing away a headache. Her eyes found me. "He's in bed."

More murmuring came from the other end, but the volume of it faded away against the changing rhythm of my heart incessantly pounding away enough so that the warm vibration of pumping blood could be heard, and felt, in my chest, in my ears, and against the sides of my head.

And my mother relented.

"Five minutes, all right?"

She covered the microphone end of the receiver with her palm and held it out in my direction.

"He wants to talk to you."

Now, I was never a bad kid; I always listened to and respected grownups because, back then, I didn't know to do anything different than what an adult said. Unlike many kids today, I didn't argue, bargain, or flat out refuse when asked or told to do something—it was an idea that never crossed my mind, or the minds of many other kids back when I was growing up. I say all of that because I believe (and if my unreliable memory serves correct) this was the first instance where I didn't do what an adult expected of me. It had nothing to do with my attitude. Quite simply, when my mother stretched the cord of the phone in my direction (from my point of view, visualize this as some bad Eighties horror movie attempt to show off the 3-D gag), I froze.

"Noah," my mother hissed. She wagged the phone. From where she was standing in the doorway the coiled white cord had been stretched almost straight. It couldn't reach me where I was on the floor in front of the TV.

Her eyes turned pleading. Ever the peacekeeper, she just wanted things to go without a hitch.

But still I didn't move.

Mom sighed, stepped out into the hall, and brought back with her the base of the phone, which came into my room far enough that the cord could now reach where I sat.

"Please, Noah," she whispered. "At the very least do this for me."

There are a handful of times as a child when you begin to see the inner-workings into how adults really make things work in the world. It's not totally beyond kids that their lives are a bit of fantasy. They have meals made for them, the skid-marks in their underwear cleaned. Their one and only true job is going to school to be educated, to become something greater than their parents. They don't pay bills. Kids, for the most part, have a secure roof over their heads, and a place to lay their head at night. All due to how Mommy and Daddy struggle to make things work.

After my father answered the call and left home for the last time, and didn't come back, I saw a glimpse of the "man behind the curtain," known in adult speak as The Real World. I saw the grittiness, the struggle. The things I wasn't supposed to see yet. Mom took on extra hours at work to make sure we could keep a roof over us, and enough groceries to keep our bellies full. I heard her argue with the electric company several times about eventually catching up to our balance, and would give what she could until we were finally squared away, just, please, don't turn the power off.

That same desperation was in her whisper to me to please accept the telephone.

I finally did, because despite what concessions she'd made in giving me up for the weekend, she needed a break. Mom wasn't the bad guy. She was just stuck in a horrible spot. Given all I had experienced by age twelve, I was old enough to realize this was one more glimpse into the true workings of the world adults inhabit, where compromise is just as valuable as money, and by accepting the phone it made my mother's life less of a deteriorating personal hell.

But I wouldn't talk to him. No way. That was asking too much. Besides, I really had nothing to say to him. I assume my father knew I had taken possession of the phone by the sound of my breathing.

HIM: Hey kiddo.

Hearing that voice for the first time in two years, and address me in such a casual way, was an assault against the wall of my indifference. I was supposed to be angry with this man, and wanted to be. He left us. He left *me*. This was my best friend. But I just couldn't let him suffer my wrath. My continued silence played more out of confusion over how I should've felt.

HIM: I can't wait to see you. Got some pretty neat stuff planned for us. You excited?

When I said nothing this second time, he started getting the hint. That lightened, airy tone he took with me dropped right off.

HIM: Put your mom back on.

I held the phone out to her.

With a displeased stare and a frown that didn't do her looks any favors, she snagged the phone out of my hand, huffed, and retreated toward my doorway. Though she was leaning out into the hall, and trying to speak softly, I heard every word.

"Well, what did you expect, Scott? You think he was just going to open right up to you?"

He must've done a lot of talking then because she went silent for a while. I remained close to the glass screen of the television. The soft blue glow gave off the tiniest hum of static that raised hairs on my head and buzzed in my ear.

"He's a different boy now." The disquieting way she said this insinuated some piece of me had been lost along the way. Mom hung up soon after and stuck her head back inside the doorway. "Bedtime."

She went downstairs, and remained down there for quite a while. I was in bed, eyes closed, but still awake when she later snuck in to kiss me on the forehead. There was the strong, sweet scent of Riesling surrounding her like an aura. She'd had much more than her ritual single glass that night. I waited until I heard her settle into bed on the other side of the wall beyond the foot of my bed before closing my eyes again.

She was asleep in no time.

I don't know how long I spent listening to the sharp February wind wrap around the eaves.

FRIDAY

When my father still lived at home he had an office to the left at the top of the stairs. I didn't much go in there when he was around—if the door was closed it meant he didn't want to be disturbed with whatever he was working on—and I went in there even less after he decided not to come home. One angry day Mom decided she wasn't giving up space in her house to someone who didn't want to be there. After boxing everything of his, the space became her sewing room.

More times than not I would catch her in there sulking. She'd be at the desk that was centered under the darkened light fixture in the ceiling, the pale orange illuminance from the tiny bulb on the sewing machine cast a shine that painted her shadow on the wall behind her, a worn out and holey pair of my school pants half fed through the machine, but her remaining still. Her hands were down at her sides, her foot away from the pedal under the desk.

I've never believed in ghosts. There just hasn't been any concrete evidence to support their existence. I do, however, believe a house can be haunted by the presence of someone who used to live there. Memories burrow into walls and floors that can't be covered up by a new carpet or a fresh coat of paint. My father very much haunted his office, much as I can assume some spirit of him also occupied their bedroom, and the bed they shared.

That morning, on my way down for breakfast, I stopped in front of that open door that once lead into his office. So many memories flooded in of the times I would pass by on mornings heading out for school, or coming up to bed at night, and seeing my father at his desk, either typing away on his computer, or talking on that special phone that was installed as a direct line just for him. He always made sure to give me a reassuring smile whenever he caught me peeking in on him.

That morning, I could almost picture him standing by the desk that used to be his. One hand on the phone, the cord wrapped around his body as he sat atop the desk, the other hand tossing me a wave.

It was my mother calling that snapped me out of the trance.

The plan was that I would be dropped off at his place around six. My father lived on the outskirts of the itsy bitsy town of Dalton, Pennsylvania. The trip would take us a little over an hour due to the increasing traffic near the NY/PA border. Dalton was the kind of place where the term "next door neighbors" meant having to drive at least a mile in either direction to the next house over. Dense woods and wide fields of long grass populated the hills and along the winding side roads, some of which consisted of loose dirt and stone. There was only one mainline drag that showcased the essentials: your basic stop-n-fuels, a few bars and *sammich* shops, and an Arby's. Everything in Dalton branched off Main Street like veins from an artery.

The sky that late Friday afternoon was a burst of fiery reds and pinks as we followed 81 South in my mother's forest green Jeep Wrangler. The sun sat a few degrees above the horizon and was shining bright through my window on the passenger side. I had to squint through the dirty smudges on the glass to see the stacks of smoke rising out of the brick chimneys of large farmhouses passing by in the blur from the highway. Aside from the occasional cough or sniffle, the majority of our ride down was encased in silence. I wasn't happy about being twelve and having no say in my weekend plans, and I think my mother didn't know how to make it any better so she didn't even try. The first time she said anything was when we passed a sign proclaiming the exit for Dalton to be twenty miles out.

"I'm sorry," she said.

It had come so abruptly I wasn't sure she'd even spoken, not until I looked over at her and saw she was looking back, possibly to ascertain some sense of forgiveness from me. A ray of light from the setting sun hit me square in the eyes as I turned away and resumed staring out my window. "About what?" I asked, as if I didn't have an inkling. My breath fogged a small section of the glass directly in front of my mouth.

She sighed. "When things . . . happened . . . with your father . . . I just . . . didn't handle them right. I got so . . . angry. How could he do this to us, you know? How many times were we just supposed to be understanding of things? How many times had he been called away—sent somewhere he couldn't tell us about, you know? How many times did he have to leave us in the blink of an eye and we didn't even know if we'd ever see him again? That we had to plan our lives around him and what he did because we never knew when that goddamned phone of his would ring again."

Hearing her rant the way she did, I wondered more as to why I wasn't more pissed off about it all. My displeasure regarding having no say in the visit that weekend has been well documented already, but, in the grand scheme of it all, I just felt more slighted than anything else. You would think I should have been more upset towards the man who hadn't made it a point over the last two years to arrange time for me, but I wasn't. A two-year absence to someone so young is fragile; it feels like a lifetime. At the young age I was, I didn't feel I really knew my father anymore, much less needed him.

"I never wanted you to feel like I was keeping you from him," my mother explained. I looked back at her. She wiped at a tear under her right eye before it had a chance to take shape and slide down the mound of her cheek. "None of this has been fair to you, and I'm sorry for that."

She composed herself. The ribbons of dusk in the changing sky—luminous and full of variety one moment—took on a monochromatic and sinister tone. The reds, oranges, and pinks had turned a cool shade of violet in the atmosphere, the landscape now black, erasing all those fields and houses in coarse shadow. The darkening of the skyward color was fitting, a sign of how I felt internally, like some astrological mood ring.

"He left both of us," I said.

The next sign to pass on the right indicated we were fifteen miles outside of Dalton.

It would be full on dark when we got there.

Once the apologetic conversation had been taken care of, my mother's demeanor shifted. What came out of her mouth next was said without even the slightest hint of question as to whether or not she was deadly serious. She was being blunt for the sake of making sure I couldn't possibly misinterpret. It did, however, make me wonder just what I was in for, and how it was she could leave me so far from home without her.

"I'll be an hour away, Noah," she said. "If, for God's sake, anything happens, you don't call me, all right?"

I kept a blank stare on her, trying to follow.

"It'll take me too long to come get you. You call 911. Understand?"

I nodded to let her know I did. I wasn't sure what it was she thought, or feared might happen, and I didn't dare ask.

Having that knowledge now . . . I should have asked.

We'd been at least ten minutes off the mainline in Dalton when Mom cut a sharp right. The Jeep began a steady climb up a rough and mostly crumbling slope of loose gravel riddled with holes. Flanking both sides of the path were woods too dark to see into. Only the frontline trunks and the very tops of the naked trees could be made out in the dying light. Silhouettes of skeletal branches jutted out to create dark cracks in the deep violet of dusk.

Though I knew civilization—and by that I mean Arby's—was just a few miles behind us back along the main stretch, it seemed we were now maneuvering through No Man's Land, a place beyond even God's reach.

Even considering the Jeep's headlights cut wide eyes through the black, there wasn't much to see of our own surroundings. There was hardly a second's worth of warning before the tires plunged through pockets of deep divots that was our road. One such unseen crater caused me to thwack the top of my head off the ceiling.

"Jesus," my mother said as we continued barreling violently through the pock-marked path. I said nothing, but my hands gripped tight—one on the seatbelt, one of the inside door handle. I was fighting all forces that threatened to launch me every which way out of my seat.

The upward climb ended, but the Swiss cheese road went on for a few more miles. Thank goodness no one came at us from the opposite direction. We were traveling down the middle of the road, traversing the loose earth and gravel, which provided the most stability, and less amount of head trauma.

"Remind me to send the bill for my shocks to your father."

Following this the pitch black opened up on the left to reveal a large square plot of open land carved out of the dense forest. Hard to make out in the night, an old three-story farmhouse, painted white (and chipping upon closer inspection) with gray shutters, stood back about one hundred yards from the road, appearing out of the gloom against the last remnants of sunset. The few lit windows peered out like eyes. Smoke billowed out of the uneven stock. A stone drive appeared just after a white mailbox with the numbers eight-one-five stickered to the side.

"I think this is it," said Mom, not sounding at all upbeat, or even slightly relieved to be off the punishing dirt road.

We pulled in and parked behind a large red Chevy pickup with a black cab cover. The lights of the Jeep put a spot on one particular bumper sticker plastered over the face of the Chevy's drop gate: I SERVED, WHAT'S YOUR EXCUSE?

Mom cut the engine. It was then I became introduced to both the vast, eerie silence that came with living out in the boondocks, and the absolute enclosure of the dark. I'd grown up and lived my entire life in town, where the night was still permeated by the sickly orange iridescent glow of the streetlamps, and the occasional engine or horn of a distant vehicle or passing train. The quiet and dark out in the countryside was absolute. This was all a culture shock. With the Jeep's engine cooling, clicking under the hood, my mother had yet to withdraw her key from the ignition, as if still not totally on board with her end of the deal with my father. It wouldn't have surprised me had she given the key a crank, shifted into reverse, and gotten us the hell out of there. Hell, I even prayed for it.

I often wonder how my life may have gone differently if she had.

"Sixty-eight hours," she said. I wasn't sure if she was saying that to me or just talking herself into following through. There came the scratch of her key dragging its teeth out of the steering column. "I'll be here at two o'clock on Monday. Not a minute later. Promise."

I nodded. Promise.

She collected my backpack out of the backseat and walked me to the door. There was a covered wraparound porch, the ceiling of which sagged in places. The waterlogged planks of the steps as well as the floorboards of the porch sighed and bent under our weight. There was the woven smell of burning cherry wood and mud and dank seeping along in the chilly February night. Mushy piles of dead leaves and dirty boot prints were scattered around in clumps all over the porch. Mom pulled open the screen door to the unwelcome tune of the coils of the spring yawning, threatening to snap. She knocked, the heavy door rattling in the jamb against the side of her fist. There was no doorbell switch to press, only two exposed wires hung where a switch plate would normally exist.

I remember wondering what my father paid for this dump.

In the frigid air my jangled nerves were obvious through each breath. Instead of a long, steady puff of steam exiting from between my lips, rising to dissipate in the night, each exhale was shaky and produced thin wisps from my trembling mouth. To try and conceal my anxiousness, I started taking breaths through my nose, long and slow—it was easier to control my breathing that way.

Before long the shape of a familiar silhouette appeared behind the slim vertical window alongside the front door. In the base of my throat I felt the turning and heavy click of the lock sliding back into its slot in the door. I awaited the inevitable with a prickling sense of finality. My mother put a supportive hand across my shoulder. Through the heavy layer of my winter coat I felt her warmth and reassurance. Sixty-seven hours and fifty-seven minutes left. The handle on the door turned.

"Well, hello there." My father flashed a pleasant smile, his eyes going back and forth between us as if he were following a tennis match. For many years, and in all of our photos at home, he sported some range of facial hair. In the warmer months he usually kept a goatee, whereas in the winter he went full on mountain man. His face when that door opened that night was completely shaven. The smile he wore revealed one deep dimple on the right side and half of one on the left. He also had a small birthmark just above the cleft of his lip on the left side that I never knew of. His eyes were large, warm, and inviting. Being a serviceman, my father also used to keep a close crop up top, but now wore a medium length of wavy auburn hair that was swept back off his forehead. A few untamed springs hung over his ears. This was a stranger standing before me.

Still, I wasn't about to let my guard down. An old beat-to-shit Ford Mustang can always get a spankin' new body—doesn't mean anything problematic under the hood has even been tinkered with.

"Hey, big guy." He scanned me up and down. He then stepped back out of the doorway. "My apologies, please come in. Freezing out there."

We stepped into a narrow foyer that was dimly lit by wall sconces. Tacky forest green wallpaper with golden etchings went from the wood baseboard to the ceiling, interrupted by a white wood border running across midway. To our immediate left inside the doorway was a naked black iron coat rack. On our right a white staircase went to a landing then cut left to additional steps to the second floor. A single bench rested near a closet door that went under the stairs. Almost at once I noticed how much stronger the smell of burning wood had become.

"You like that?" my father asked. "It's cherry wood. The previous owners kept a small room in the basement stocked to the ceiling with it. Already chopped and stacked. Must be close to a thousand dollars' worth down there."

My mother sniffed audibly, and didn't seem impressed. "I smell meat."

My father snapped his fingers. "That would be the burgers." In a haste he was away from us, walking briskly down the short hall and through a swinging door into the kitchen. My mother and I exchanged glances. He reappeared halfway out the swinging doorway a moment later, a metal spatula pasted with charred bits of meat was wielded in his right hand. "Burgers are about done. If you guys want to take the self-guided tour you're more than welcome. Noah—" he pointed to the stairs with the spatula "—your room is up and to the left. Follow the hall, last door on the right if you want to take your stuff up." He then eyed Mom. "Maggie, there's plenty of grub if you want to stay."

Before she could answer he was gone again. The kitchen door swung to and fro in his wake before settling on the hinges.

"Go ahead," Mom urged. "I'll help your father."

That was code for me to go on alone—she had something brewing on her mind that was moments from exiting her mouth. I shouldered my bag and beat feet up the stairs.

The top of the staircase ended in the middle of a hall. The ceiling was high, walls painted a bland taupe. No frames or other décor hung for display in either direction. I found my room. The inside was lit, the door had been left cracked, waiting. There was a made bed—the headboard up against the right-side wall—resting atop a burgundy area rug. A small adjustable lamp on the bedside table cast shallow light that spread long shadows from the furniture over the dark-stained floor. There was a short, two-tier bookshelf that sat empty under a windowsill on the far side. The dresser up against the left wall looked like a thrift shop special with its scratches and scuffs, but was real wood not balsa. A fresh can of stain sat on the floor next to it. On top of the dresser were two cans of paint, two brand new brushes, a clean white roller, and a note. I dropped my bag onto the bed and went over to read the folded piece of paper standing up against the first paint can.

Walls are a bit plain. Maybe a little color can help make this space yours.

The four walls looked to have been primed already, a fairly discernable odor of the cover-up chemical clung to the room. I checked the label on the paint bucket and saw he chose a shade called Dill. Surprised me that he remembered my favorite color was green.

At the same moment I returned the note to dresser top, the heightened voice of my mother came traveling up through the heating vent beneath the floor grate by my feet. I figured the vent must have shared with a downstairs room near the kitchen or dining room.

". . . and you're just gonna go on pretending with him that nothing ever happened?"

I knelt down and lowered my ear to the grate. Besides them I could hear—and smell—the burgers cooking. The grease sizzled on the stove.

My father retorted, slightly snarky, slightly agitated, but nowhere near upset: "No, Maggie, I'm not just gonna pretend nothing happened, but what do you want me to do? I thought it might be a bit too much to start out our weekend groveling and begging for forgiveness a minute after he walked in the door."

Mom: It's not like he's oblivious, Scott. Noah . . . (Sighs) . . . He's quiet. He's a *feeling* boy. He's not just going to come out and tell you he's upset.

Him: Besides the fact that you're describing my kid to me like I don't know who he is—and yes, even with all the horrible things I've done, I haven't forgotten what kind of person Noah is—what leads you to believe he is so upset about all of this?

Mom: . . .

Him: You know what I think? I think *you're* the one who's upset most about this weekend.

Mom: (Raised voice) That's because on the phone you made it sound so goddamn urgent, Scott! You were so demanding to see him, and so upset because he wouldn't talk to you. Then we show up and you're all smiles and good manners and flipping burgers.

Him: (Snapping) Maybe it's because we all don't need a constant reminder of what happened!

Silence. The grease popped.

Him: (Cooling a bit) Yeah, I messed up, and I'm paying for it. I want forgiveness—from Noah, from you—but I know I don't deserve it yet. I haven't earned it. I know we have to start over. I want to gain his trust. And yours.

Mom: (Softly) You want to know how I know your son is upset about all of this, Scott? Because he *doesn't* say anything about it.

She was right. And while I wished I could have seen the looks on their faces during this exchange, I was glad they couldn't see the one on my own.

Mom: What is it you're not telling me?

She must have seen something in his face. A twitch of the eye, a brief scowl, something to clue her in.

Him: Nothing.

Mom: You're just like him. Neither of you talk when something's really bothering you. But if whatever is going on that I don't know about has anything to do with Noah—

Him: We can't talk about this now.

Mom: (A flare of her earlier agitation) And why the hell not?

Him: Is he up in his room?

Mom: He went up to the room you set for him, yeah.

My father didn't bother lowering his voice for me not to hear.

Him: His room shares this heating duct.

My mother said nothing. I imagined her shrugging, failing to see what that had to do with anything.

Him: He can hear us.

Silence.

Pop and sizzle.

Trying not to create a sound and make my eavesdropping any more known, I backed away from the grate and flopped onto the bed. The old mattress had a lot of give. It swallowed me up nearly whole. The worn springs groaned and creaked. My thoughts wandered, eyes locked on the ceiling. There wasn't anything further from my folks until I was summoned for dinner. Till then there was my Game Gear to provide distraction.

I tried my best not to linger on whatever it was my father didn't say. Whatever was bothering him, according to my mother in their conversation.

What he didn't want me, or her, to know.

My mother opted not to stick around for dinner. I don't believe she had any intention of doing so to begin with, and I think since she believed my father should have been down on his knees busy with repenting rather than putting on smiles and an apron, added to the already sour taste in her mouth. She took me aside in the foyer, said her byes, kissed me on the forehead, told me to behave in a volume to catch my father within earshot, and then whispered for me to be careful and to remember what she said in the car (*911*), before she was out the door into the frozen night.

The closing of the door behind her sounded and felt louder than it likely was.

Just the two of us then. My father invited me to join him in the dining room.

Covering the table was quite the delectable spread. A blue porcelain plate of charred burgers was centered among the dishes of sides that included diced red onions, slices of American cheese, romaine lettuce, and thinly-sliced beefsteak tomatoes. The fries were served jungle style in a basket lined with wax paper. Prior to this meal, I'd never known my father to have a skill in culinary; Mom made all our meals when it was the three of us. She had a hard time with easy staples, like mac and cheese.

For the longest stretch we ate in silence; the crunch of the fries and munching through burger rolls with onion and lettuce was the soundtrack of our dinner. It was my father who eventually disturbed this stretch of disquiet.

"I'm sorry you had to hear all of that earlier."

A large hunk of burger and bread was stuffed inside my cheek, which was a relief because I clearly wasn't able to retort. To maintain this inability so speak, I stopped chewing and listened, as he had more to say.

"May be hard for you to believe when you consider everything," he said, lifting his glass of water and sipping off the top, "but the last thing I wanted was to upset your mother. Lord knows I'm good at it, though."

A buildup of saliva forced me to resume chewing and swallow down hard the lumps of mashed food. I still didn't respond. He went back to picking at his fries.

Reminiscent of our phone conversation the night prior, I wracked my brain in search for something to say, but some long-buried stubbornness was quite all right with me never uttering a word, as if I had a point to prove. Maybe he deserved my eternal silence. Problem is I've never had a long-term follow through when actually faced with a difficult situation. Just not in my nature to carry a grudge. I'd have to say something eventually.

And sure enough it came out not long after we resumed our meal at the dinner table.

"Are you dying?" I asked. My voice was raw with nary a hint of remorse.

The remainder of my father's burger—a quarter's worth—held by three fingers in his right hand and hovering a few inches below his open mouth was returned to the plate. His brow flexed. "What makes you ask something like that?"

"You haven't been around," I said. The remnants of my own food sat untouched on the plate, my hunger gone. "You missed my birthday twice, and Christmas, and everything else. I guess why else would you want to see me?"

For the first time in my life, at the age of twelve, I got to witness what it looks like when someone falls completely apart on the inside. It looked as if two invisible hands reached through my father's back and strangled every organ at once, squeezing and twisting out their juices like a person would wring out a soaked t-shirt or towel. His body withdrew from the table, his eyes blinking unfathomably. My words hit a nerve. Good.

He composed himself quickly.

"Noah," he said. "There are a lot of things you don't know. Some pretty horrible things happened the last time I got called away.

"I've made mistakes," he continued after a moment, "a lot of them, all of them insurmountable in my eyes, and I know you heard a little about that. Again, I'm sorry you had to hear it that way. But . . . this is a chance for us. For me to right the wrongs. Not erase them or forget them, but move on from them. That's what I want out of this weekend. I want you back."

He left it at that for me to digest, along with what burger and fries and grease already weighed heavy in my stomach, sloshing around. He got up, collected the dishes, and took them out to the sink.

In the end, he didn't lie to me. He wanted forgiveness and reconciliation. But there was more. He knew it being so early into our visit which truths to avoid telling me.

For instance, it wasn't long after he got up that I realized he didn't even answer my original question.

My father did the dishes and I went upstairs to give my Game Gear some attention. After about thirty minutes I heard the running faucet quit. I held a bit of guilt over avoiding him but, like my mother, I sensed something unsettled in him, something dark.

Shortly after he finished up in the kitchen, there came the sound of heavy footfalls ascending the staircase. I paused my game of Sonic and thumbed down the volume dial, waiting to hear which direction my father would take once he reached the second floor hall. There was a long hesitation after the groan of the last stair faded off into quiet. I pictured him unsure which direction to take, looking left which led down to my room, and then right where he would follow the hall down to his own bed. He took his time deciding. I counted each thudding heartbeat in the meantime.

If he went left, he potentially faced an awkward situation. If he went right, or back down the stairs, it would be a continuation of his past mistakes.

When his steps resumed, they were in my direction.

I flipped the power switch and stored the Game Gear under my pillow, unsure how my father would handle my retreating upstairs to play videogames. He stopped outside the door and knocked. The door opened gently about a foot. My father peeked his head in.

"Just heading down to bed. I know it's a little early yet, but I'm usually up early."

I said nothing.

He remained there as if caught in a struggle. Without looking at me, he entered the room, strolled over and took a seat at the foot of the bed next to my feet. He remained leaning forward, elbows on thighs, his hands folded in front of his mouth. When he moved his hands away he sighed the words "Midnight Star" with heavy emphasis.

My forehead wrinkled. "Huh?"

My father kept his eyes trained on the floor. I observed his hands. They were clasped, fingers wringing. He still wore his wedding band, and went about twisting it just below the knuckle. "That was the name of my mission. Midnight Star.

"We had been sent to this city deep in the Middle East. Some high profile targets the CIA had been keeping tabs on for years had been identified in the area. Some high-rankers in our government thought it made for a great opportunity to take out a lot of dangerous people in one fell swoop. So they sent us in."

"That's when you left?" I asked, referring to when I was ten and his office phone last rang.

He nodded, and finally looked at me.

"These were bad people, Noah. I want you to know that. They—the government high-rankers—thought an airdrop was too risky in such a concentrated area. They wanted boots on the ground. They wanted eyeballs on these guys to ID them quickly when they were dead. And they wanted the least amount of collateral damage possible. Most of all, they wanted it done quiet so news organizations wouldn't catch wind until long after we were back on our way home, at the very least.

"We arrived in the city at night by helicopter. My team and I staked out a house believed to be where these terrorists were meeting from the rooftop of an abandoned building down the road. It was hard to see anything. The windows had been covered with thick drapes. Our intel had been certain, but we weren't willing to take the chance had they been keeping innocents as shields. Such a thing isn't uncommon to these people.

"A few hours passed. The sun started coming up, and we needed to decide quick: It was either do what we had been brought in to do, or leave." He took a deep breath, let it out. The weight of his breathing indicated he was still rummaging through the strain of that decision that had long ago been made. "Unfortunately, there's no simple answer, and us guys in Special Forces don't do the things we can't live with. Leaving felt wrong. Shooting up a potential hostage spot wasn't our deal either. So we stayed, and tried our best to hide inside the building and get as much intel as we could. Once the sun was up we could do nothing but wait. Air support was hundreds of miles away on a freighter. They couldn't come in under full daylight. We were on our own.

"We spent the next day huddled inside the vacant building while a few of our own dressed in thaubs and canvased the road. They were trying to gain any intel on whether the men we were there for were still around in the building we'd been watching. I was staked out in a window on the top floor, keeping watch through a scope on a rifle. I had to be ready for anything."

He cleared his throat.

"For a while nothing happened. We'd even begun to wonder if the mission hadn't been created out of falsified reports."

His expression turned grimmer.

"Then came the boy."

I blinked. "Boy?"

"He wasn't much older than you are now. He came out of the building we'd been staking. I watched him down the barrel of the scope coming closer to my guys. He just came out and was walking a straight line. Odd. His face was pale. Blank. I'll never get it out of my head.

"He was mumbling something. Couldn't make it out. My guys started talking to him, calling out. They were saying stop, to not come closer. But . . . he just ignored them."

"What was wrong with him?" I asked, aloof to a horror that has become commonplace. My father never acknowledged my naivety. He let it last a moment, likely knowing full well what he was about to share would kill off a large part of my innocence as to how I viewed the world. "Did he not understand English?"

"I believe he understood my men," my father said. "They shouted to him in many languages to try and reach him, but, Noah, this boy . . . he was being sent to kill us."

I remember thinking this didn't seem possible. How could a child kill soldiers?

"Under his garments," my father explained, "there were explosives taped to his body. Someone had turned him into a walking bomb. They were hoping because he was a child we would let him get close to us, then . . . they would detonate."

I started to feel sick. "What happened to him?"

A breath. "I prayed," my father said. "Hadn't done that in forever." His eyes welled up. "I didn't want to do it but I had to. It wasn't even a choice, which is what makes it so unfair." He turned to me, face as white as a wraith. "I killed that boy."

My stomach turned. Muscles cramped. My food sat ugly, roiling inside.

"I had him in my sights and, in one shot, it was over."

Neither of us said anything for a while, both in shock over the admission. I turned it all over in my young mind, trying to wrap my head around the facts and the implications.

From that moment, I lived in a world where children had been—and continued to be—turned into weapons. Monsters saw no value in them as people, but their potential for dealing out deadly acts. Soldiers were now faced with having to do the unspeakable. Like the skin coming off an apple, a protective layer that kept me from the harsher truths of the world had been peeled away, leaving the delicate inside to slowly go to spoil. And like an apple, the world was dangerous and poisonous at its core.

I lived with this pessimistic view right up to when my daughter was born. And it was with her birth that the despicable act my father committed really hit home.

When I first lay eyes on my daughter in the delivery room, although she was caked head to toe in an oil slick of dark and crusty blood, along with globs of yellow and white mucus and other fluids I couldn't identify, I had never seen anything more beautiful, and so precious. It was inalienable and immeasurable love at first sight. The experience of her birth changed me. Awakened me. I used to be more carefree, angrier in my teen years and twenties. More liberal, too, about my beliefs. Looking back, I consider that period to be a very "unfocused" time of my life. The long weekend with my father had been the catalyst.

But when I held my daughter for the first time, I came to understand three things.

First, I will never know how my father conjured whatever he did (I wouldn't call it *bravery* because I don't think he would agree) that made him pull the trigger on that boy. Perhaps he would call it a desperate sense of self-preservation. Regardless, I don't think I could have done what he did. Having a child of my own made me extremely emotional towards anything that had to do with children. I couldn't watch a film, or read a book where a child was to be harmed. I could also produce intense worry and tears at the drop of a hat, whereas before such things had been foreign to me.

Second, looking into my daughter's eyes, I became inspired with hope. Hope that I can make a better future for her, and that she'll get a better childhood than I did. Which leads into the third thing I learned when my daughter was born . . .

There had been a deep-seeded fear within me while growing up that, someday, I would become my father.

When I held my baby girl in the delivery room as my wife was getting stitched up, and came to my understandings, I got a flash in my head of the moment I almost had to kill my father in order to save my own life.

But before that fateful portion of our weekend came to fruition, the conversation we had been having took an unexpected turn.

"I ever tell you about the day you were born, Noah?"

I gave him a subtle shake of my head.

"You were ten days late. Your mom and I spent the night in the hospital—your mom labored for twenty-four hours. Nurses joked that you were content just where you were." He spoke this with a growing smile during his reminisce. "The doctor decided on a caesarian to get you out.

"While they prepped your mom in the OR, I had been out in the hall trying to be calm and sit in a chair, but my legs were restless, my hands were clammy. When they brought me in they directed me to sit right next to your mom's head. I held her hand.

"The doctors kept telling us what was happening. They saw you. Said you had the most beautiful set of eyebrows they'd ever seen."

I smiled at this. Couldn't help it. Such an odd thing to compliment.

"Then, when they got you out, they held you up over the sheet so we could see you for the first time. I cried."

He was fighting tears even then.

"The doctors put you on a heated table to clean you up and get your vitals. I got to meet you first. I gave you my hand. You stopped crying. You just kind of stared at my hand for a while, then you tried feeding on my fingers."

A quiet laugh slipped out of him. This was the first moment in our time reunited that I felt at ease in the presence of my father.

"They were right, you know," he said. "You did have beautiful eyebrows."

I could see the tears holding in the corners of his eyes as he looked at me, studied me. This moment between us was allowed to simmer. Then, he looked away.

"Somewhere out there is a father, whose little boy I took away from him. I don't believe the father was the one that strapped the bomb to him . . . what father could do that?"

There was no answer to this.

"When I came back home from that mission . . . nothing felt right. I wanted nothing more than to be with you and Mom . . . but . . . I didn't feel like I deserved it."

The moment between us cooled, dimmed.

"I couldn't drag you two into my hell."

He regarded me again with his tear-stricken eyes.

"I am truly sorry, Noah."

He then stood from the bed. He edged his way out into the hall, wishing me goodnight before closing the door behind him. I waited until I could no longer hear the sound of his footsteps drifting off down the far side of the hall before I lay my head.

I didn't sleep for a long time. I kept thinking about how my mother would feel had she learned the things I had been told. Would she forgive him? Drop her grudge?

I was surprised to find I'd been well on my way already.

My father also didn't go right to bed. After a while of quiet, there came the sound of a door creaking open on the other side of the house. I could hear him climb two short stacks of stairs. Then he was above me, in the attic, crossing the floor. Not exactly pacing. It sounded as if something heavy was being dragged around. Something else that was long was then draped across the floor. What was he working on?

My eyes eventually grew heavy listening to him. I don't know how long he stayed up, but it was just after three in the morning when I awoke to the sound of his screams.

SATURDAY

I awoke thinking someone was in the house with us.

Opening your eyes in a new place—a place you're not accustomed to—can be startling enough. It took my mind a moment to recalibrate to my surroundings (*This isn't my room . . . this isn't my house*). What didn't help dispel my fears that I was living a nightmare was the sounds of pure hell that dragged me out of sleep.

The bedside clock read seven after three as the cries started up again.

From the far side of the house came a series of agonized wails. My hands clutched to the comforter around me, then wrapped around my ears in response to the terror that otherwise froze me on the spot. It sounded like someone was torturing my father. Never before that night had I ever heard such a sound. It was awful. Unfathomable. Alien.

I actually prayed for it to end. Prayed that if someone was actually killing him that they just get it over with. Prayed then that they wouldn't find me.

But the sounds only intensified, coming and going every few moments, going on far too long and with no other sounds in between. At the height of my fear I would have heard something else, anything else. My hearing was so attuned in that moment where I believed his life, and my own, was at stake. And yet there was nothing else. That's when I knew it was only him in his room producing that sound. But why was beyond comprehension.

I didn't care to find out, but I wasn't prepared for the pull—a combination of anger and concern that eventually flared within me.

My mother said to call 911 should anything happen. Getting out of bed to locate a telephone was a lost notion. My entire body was wracked with locked muscles. My knees were drawn up to my chest under the comforter. I pressed my hands tighter against my ears, and just kept begging for it to end (*Stop. Please stop.*). His howls of despair had drilled in too deep. They were inside my head cackling away. Bouncing around like the echoes in a cave, or the tortured moans of a poltergeist wandering the desolate halls of an old abandoned house. My teeth hurt from clenching my jaw so tight. Gooseflesh flared like a rash all over my skin. His damned cries just wouldn't end.

My fear quickly turned over to anger.

I kept telling myself that at any moment he would wake himself and the noises would stop, but they didn't. He only got louder. I cursed him under my breath, eyes open and fixed on the bedroom door, my voice trembling, willing him, telling him to just fucking stop!

I threw off the covers.

There was a tightening in my chest that came with getting off that bed. It was as if my father and I had become magnets, and I could feel the draw, the pull toward him. We'd made some sort of connection over the talk he had with me—the boy he murdered, how he remembered everything from when I was born. I tried not to be angry, tried to maintain a sense of compassion.

It was easier to be angry.

The chill in the room clasped over my clammy skin, constricting the back of my shirt where sweat had caked the clothing to my body. My bare feet touched down on the area rug and I went for the door.

In the dark of the hall, in the middle of the witching hours, when all other disturbances cease to exist, the irregular sounds of the house had awakened and come out to play. The stretching and settling of the walls, the creaking of old windows and eaves and siding, the grunting of the floors, all of it seeped into my ears, playing tricks in my head. Every slow step in advancement of my father's room caused more of the old house's aches and pains to vocalize. If the house itself was trying to compel me to turn back, I would have believed it, and probably should have listened. Still, I kept on. The pull, and my rising anger, was that strong.

Finally, I reached his room.

The door was partially open. A gentle push was all it needed to give me a glimpse of the horror taking place inside.

Cast in a muted shade of dull moonlight coming in the window on the right was my father stretched out over his bed. His lean, sweaty torso was exposed—the patchwork quilt cast aside in a pile on the floor. The top sheet was twisted around his lower half as he writhed on his back in the throes of what appeared to be a fairly searing nightmare.

I wondered if his dreams were being haunted by that boy.

My father's arms, tattooed from shoulder to wrist with sleeves of barbed-wire that laced like a dancer's shoes, flexed as he dug handfuls into the mattress. There were red flowers drawn sporadically among the barbed-wire ink. I wasn't aware if the flowers meant anything or were just part of the design. Strands of blue veins stood out along the inside of his forearms with each clenching fist. His breathing labored husky between pained cries as his head swung side to side. His eyes were squeezed shut against some dark, overpowering force.

Whatever he saw in his dream wasn't letting go.

That boy . . . was my father envisioning the killing over and over again?

My psychiatrist once told me hell—*true* hell—was repetition.

I couldn't keep watching. I had to do something.

Seeing this reminded me of what my father used to do whenever my mother fell asleep on the couch and started to snore. Her long drags of breath through thin nasal passages produced a thick sound akin to a clunky old weed-whacker trying to saw through a tree trunk. To save our ears, and our sanity, my father would nudge her. Mom would then readjust, still asleep, and the snoring abated. That's all I had hoped to do that night—reset him.

With trepidation, I went to his bedside. Soon as my shaky hand went out, and was inches from landing against a drawn barb on his tatted shoulder, he moved with a jerk, and I startled back, my arm flinging away and nearly knocking over the lamp on the table. I wasn't going to try that again.

I decided ultimately that the safest way to initiate the reset in my father was to wake him completely, and do so by turning on the lamp at his bedside. I just hoped he wouldn't be too mad. Though I was ready to accept mad versus his continued screams.

I reached under the shade, found the small knob on the lamp's neck, and turned it until the bulb popped on soft with a *shick*. My eyes squinted in the new light. They also found the object sitting next to the base of the lamp that I had been unable to spot in the dark. At the time I didn't know the details about makes and models, but I knew a gun when I saw one. The sight of the smooth black metal of my father's SIG stopped me cold. No sooner did I look to my father—his cries had ceased—to discover his eyes were open.

I stumbled back, hands up in surprise. "Dad . . ."

It was the first time since he left home that I spoke that word. I had almost said it once before. It had been about eight months prior to the weekend visit, on the afternoon of my twelfth birthday. I'd gotten home from school and was eager to get the mail. Never before had I bothered to check the open cardboard box under the door slot that served to catch whatever the mailman brought us, but on that day I went sifting through to find anything with my name on it. In the box there were six envelopes in total, all business sized, all white. Four were bills addressed to my mother from credit card companies and utility businesses. One envelope had been made out to her—Mrs. Margaret Adams—from the Red Cross with a letter inside about donating again sometime soon because they missed her and there was a special need for her blood type. The last was a throwaway offer to win a free car and it was addressed to "Current Resident."

No birthday card from him. Nada. Zilch.

When I handed over the mail, disappointment evident, Mom asked if I had been expecting something.

I almost answered with *Dad didn't send a card*, but instead went with: "He forgot my birthday."

It was from then onward that I pretended he didn't exist. He couldn't hurt me that way.

When the word dropped out of my mouth that night at his bedside it felt foreign, like I had made it up.

As for my father, despite his eyes being open, he didn't seem to notice me. He wasn't even looking at me, just staring at the ceiling. His breathing had regained a slower rhythm. His wailing and thrashing had ended. It was as if the light on the stand had chased it all away. His torso retained a fair amount of perspiration, but his muscles were relaxed. He was at ease. The stare in his eyes remained blank.

He was asleep. It was the only thing that made sense. Somehow he was still deep under but with his eyes open.

That was enough for me. I decided to make a quick exit. Didn't even bother with the lamp.

To my complete surprise and utter gratefulness, the floorboards didn't make a sound as I slid backwards in a slow, cautious approach toward the hall. Once beyond the threshold, I thought it best to leave the door open—no reason to risk the old hinges possibly alerting him—and I had just about cleared the doorway when the bedsprings groaned and I saw my father sit straight up, looking at me.

I froze. If my bladder had been full I would have pissed myself.

My father said nothing. He didn't acknowledge me in any way. I could only figure then that he was still asleep. Even as his legs swung out over the left side of the bed, the same side where the table was with the gun, and planted his bare feet on the floor.

Needless to say, I bolted. No longer concerned with being heard, I dashed down that darkened hall with no care for what I couldn't see. Memory took over, telling me where my room was. Thankfully I managed to avoid the left side where the wall opened up to the stairs leading down.

I was careful not to slam the bedroom door, but out of twanging nerves that made any action impossible to silence, the door met the jamb pretty hard. Within seconds I was scrambling under the comforter, trying to remain as still and as quiet as possible. Quiet enough that I could hear whatever was going to happen next.

For a while there was nothing, just the sound of the crisp wind pressing hard on the windows and the walls. But then, beneath that, quiet at first, almost subliminal, there came the creaking slow-moving steps that gained volume and weight as they stalked a path in my direction.

Sure enough, he came for me.

"No . . ." I whispered with a tremble, grinding my teeth to fight the sobs. My jaw pressed together so tight it was a wonder my teeth didn't crack and dissolve into fine powder. Hot, fresh tears rolled down over the pillow, absorbing into the pillowcase. In a bizarre, yet poetic twist of fate, it was now I who was gripping handfuls of the bedsheets. Every muscle tensed. I broke out in a cold sweat.

Once I was able to calm my gasping breaths, and the pounding of my heart lulled in my ears, there came the creaking of plodding steps just outside my door.

There was nothing I could do but listen to those steps pause and remain as still as possible at the turn of the handle.

With my eyes squeezed shut, I could see it all happen inside my head. I pictured my father, still sleepwalking, his eyes still maintaining that stoic gaze, stepping inside the room. I felt him approach the bed. Even in the dark his shadow fell over me. And he remained there, hovering, for the longest time. Watching me, yet watching nothing. I could hear every breath of his draw in and let out slowly, perversely. Fighting every survival instinct crying out for me to flee made those long moments much more unbearable. Survival was not about fighting my way out; it was about not moving an inch, and silencing every breath.

I kept picturing the gun in his hand.

If I had died then, it terrifies me to think I would have gone out whimpering.

A series of muffled steps over the area rug told me he was finally moving off. Fresh tears sprung from my eyes in overwhelming relief.

Once I'd heard him far enough down the hall I leapt from the bed, closed the door, and went for the nearest piece of heavy furniture in the room. The empty dresser slid easily enough once the drawers were removed. I pushed it up tight against the door, reloading the drawers for maximum weight. Then, for good measure, I stacked the short bookcase on top, along with the paint can.

In bed I sat nestled up against the headboard, keeping watch. I didn't hear him again that night; it was a while though before I let my guard down.

I finally allowed my eyes to close once the first cracks of dawn appeared in the sky.

I hadn't drifted off for very long. My sleep was shallow, and ineffective. I opened my eyes very much exhausted, but also still on high alert. Bright rays of sun reached in through the window, spotlighting the dust particles that hung in the air. The sun seemed especially bright shining off the snow blanketing the yard—I shielded my eyes looking out.

The house was silent. Those random noises of joints and boards shifting about—the dead-of-night noises—had been driven away like a vampire at the emergence of daybreak.

Quiet as possible, I removed the bookshelf, the dresser, and the paint can away from the door. Venturing out into the hall, I listened for my father. Part of me wanted to sneak downstairs and find the phone to dial home.

There was a dense chill, thick with the stench of mildew, standing in the hall. Curious, I continued past the stairs. The air got colder. The stale stink of the hall grew heavier, tangible enough to taste.

My father's door was wide open. I peeked in to find him asleep, buried among a heap of covers that had once been wound up in bundles on the floor. He was lightly snoring, a bare leg stuck out and hung over the side. From the doorway I spotted the gun had been returned to its place on the nightstand, if it ever left there at all. I chose not to linger, slinking on.

Ten feet ahead the hall cut to the right. After making the turn it was there, about another ten feet ahead, that the hallway came to an end. I arrived at the source of the cold, and the damp smell.

A single door stood open, beyond which were three steps up to a landing beneath the slope of the roof that made the standing room about four feet. More steps continued up on the right. I recalled the sounds of my father wandering, pacing around the attic as I dozed off the night before. The sound of something long being slumped across the floor. Something heavy.

A child's mind—innocent, yet also a tad sheltered—allows for them to explore all their mild curiosities. As adults we know better. If it were now, I know I would not feel the slightest desire to investigate that attic. Perhaps I say that knowing what ghastly discovery was to be found, unlike then. Regardless, all of the accumulated fears of a lifetime prepare you to avoid situations you're not ready to confront—a tingling "Spidey-sense" if you will. But at twelve, I wanted to know if there was anything cool up there.

Despite a fit of shivering, I began the ascent. The slope of the roof and exposed trusses required me to crouch at the landing—my father had to be almost crawling at this point. To the right were three more steps up to a subfloor, where the attic expanded in all directions, allowing me to stand without worry of knocking my head. Exposed beams, collar ties, and joints crossed far above me, all of them coated in dust and vacant, worn out cobwebs. The water-stained subfloor didn't extend to the entire attic. It ceased around the fringes where the vertical space was less than three feet. There was a single window to my left, that started at about floor level, catching the sun. The place seemed like any old attic, nothing special, until I spotted the hundred or so butterflies.

They weren't real. They were decorations, synthetic insects hanging from the rafters by what I could only assume was fishing line or a thin string I couldn't see too well. The details of their wings looked magnificent from my view at the floor. There were all kinds on display—monarchs, painted ladies, mourning cloaks, swallowtails, and queens. A few swayed with the minor breaths of winter air slipping through the tiny gaps and broken seals that'd undoubtedly worn through the weaker spots of the roof over the years.

The other thing I noticed upon counting the butterflies was the pictures.

They were set up all over—photos in an assortment of frames. Some were on the floor, some on top of boxes and crates. A few were placed together up high, sitting on overhead beams. A few also sat on a worktable near the single window.

The pictures were all from times when our family was still together. Some were of me and Mom, some of me and Dad, some of just them together, a few of all of us. One in particular had me, quite a bit younger, standing in a diaper and t-shirt next to my father as he showed me one of his pressed uniforms decorated with attached medals.

It dawned on me why I hadn't seen any such pictures hanging around my father's house. He'd been keeping them all in the attic, turning it into some kind of shrine.

But I didn't know why.

Why hide all of these memories, especially when it was only he that lived here? My mother's hiding of the photographs at home made a little more sense to me then—it was for the benefit of both of us.

A closer look at the foldout worktable centered on the floor revealed a spread of loose photographs—four-by-sixes and five-by-eights—that my father hadn't framed. There were also a few loose butterflies he hadn't bothered stringing up. There was also a rope.

It was laid on the floor in a circular pile behind the table. I only spotted it as I had gotten closer. One end of the thick rope was knotted around a short leg of the table. I didn't think much of it until I walked around and picked it up. It was long and quite hefty, very similar to the kind we had to climb in order to reach the ceiling in gym class. Parts of the length were frayed. It looked to come from an old barn (maybe even the garage on the side of the house) and had been used with a pulley to lift hay bales. As I picked it up, the rope's origin didn't matter. What rang all sorts of alarms inside my head was that the opposite end had come free of the pile, and featured a string of thick knots leading to a perfect loop.

My stomach dropped upon realizing I was holding the noose my father had fashioned for himself.

I then looked around and understood at once the ghastly nature of the shrine.

My parents met a few months before they graduated high school. They both attended the old North High in Serling Oaks before it was torn down. They attended all four years but, being among twelve hundred other students occupying the building, could never once recall laying eyes on each other until their sentence was nearly over. And when they did come face to face it wasn't even on school grounds but as part of a social club run through the school, a community service project called The Well-wishers. The group had been the brainchild of a faculty member in the Social Students and Economics department for any seniors still in need of service hours that was required before walking across the stage and getting that diploma with your name on it. No teacher on the senior team wanted any repeaters the following year.

For their community project, The Well-wishers constructed a butterfly farm at one of the local parks. My parents met in the midst of a swarm of monarchs on a sunny Saturday morning in early June, 1975. They were married three years later. At the close of the ceremony tying them together as husband and wife till death did them part, they released a pair of monarchs into the sky.

Given that one of the monarchs was snatched almost immediately by a passing crow, one wonders if anyone in attendance saw that as an omen.

I supposed (much later on in life, after learning of their history together) the faux butterflies hanging in the attic was a sort of tribute—my father's way of keeping my mother with him in his solitude during the bleaker times he endured throughout his stay in that old farmhouse in Dalton.

Once I realized I was holding the very item my father had fashioned to end his own life, whatever contents remained in my stomach nearly ejected onto the floor. Through some stroke of control, I managed to set the rope back without painting the floor or worktable with what sat uneasy in my belly and got the hell out of there without creating too much noise.

In my mind, if I had made it past his door without waking him, my father wouldn't have known that I'd seen what he'd been working on.

Imagine then my complete and utter dread when I crept past his door only to peek in and find he was no longer in bed. The blankets and patchwork quilt were neatly tucked in; the pillows arranged evenly at the headboard.

In panic mode, my thought process told me if I just made it back to my room everything would be fine.

But that's where he was, waiting for me. My father was sitting on the bed, facing the door, dressed in thick workman's overalls and holding a matching canvas coat. He showed no signs of surprise, nor anger. Instead he bared a face that was blank, passive.

It felt like forever before he spoke to me. I believed I was in for it. Instead . . .

"Grab your coat, and dress in layers. We're going out."

He stood and walked out past me without a second look or another word. His cadence of steps down the hall and down the stairs was calm, steady. Just as passive as his face.

An awful feeling settled over me. A sense of not only impending doom for my father, but for the both of us.

I sensed rather quickly my father wasn't going to mention the attic. For the longest time while driving he didn't say anything. I came to learn that weekend that both my parents were awesome at maintaining long stretches of awkward silences during car rides. I'm not sure what I expected out of him but not that he was going to ignore that I'd found the place he had planned to off himself (if, indeed, he had still been planning it). The whole ride made me queasy. Plus, I was starving. He'd brought along a box of strawberry Pop-Tarts that sat between us unopened on the seat, but I didn't want to be presumptuous.

We'd gotten into his pickup, windows glazed over with frost. The cranked heat eventually bored two holes through the frost, and they expanded, finally providing enough of a view that my father felt comfortable enough pulling down the shift column and getting us on our way. Wherever it was, I wondered, we were off to.

The heat blowing through the vents never felt too warm—swear I could see the evidence of my breath for miles as we dug deeper into the Pennsylvania countryside. He drove us beyond where there were power-lines and into lands of dark forests and dormant farmlands; all the view was of wide open, snow-covered vistas, bare trees that swayed in the sharp wind, and rolling hills.

Peering out the passenger side window at the dunes of untouched snow, my thoughts continued drifting back to the attic. If my father had still been meaning to put a lasso around his neck, and he knew that I knew of his plot, then why the sudden excursion out into the middle of the ass-end of nowhere?

That sense of impending doom wrapped tighter around the tubes of my guts, cutting off the desire for one of those packages of Pop-Tarts.

"Sorry 'bout the heat," my father said to break the silence. His eyes searched for something as we became surrounded on both sides by dense forest. "Been meaning to have the truck looked at and tuned up. Been a little busy at home."

No shit, I thought.

"We're not far," he said. "Road is somewhere up here on the left."

That road came up after three more miles. No marker or sign of any kind to identify it. It wasn't even a road by the standards we hold, more of a path that looked to have been created by numerous heavy vehicles carving a way between the trees. We left behind the cracked asphalt for a narrow trail of dirt and rocks under a dark canopy of pine and naked branches.

"One day last year I just went out driving," my father said. His eyes didn't so much as wince with each thwack of a dangling branch being snapped off the windshield. Mine did. "This was just before the winter got cold enough to completely freeze over the lakes and streams. It had snowed about four inches the night before, and I happened to spot this trail. I know it doesn't look like much now, but when you see where we're going it'll all be worth it."

The front tires rolled over a patch of pockmarks in the earth, pitching me around the seat. Déjà vu. I worried for my head and the ceiling above me. My father never slowed, shocks be damned. The truck rumbled on through the uneven pits despite the hell it had to be wreaking on the frame.

"Pop-Tart?" my father offered.

I shook my head. Didn't think I could stomach one.

"You look nervous, Noah. Like you think I brought you all the way out here just to leave you." A person joking around would have cracked a grin, winked, or at the very least mentioned they were just kidding around. My father remained stone cold even.

The undercarriage of the truck clanged and rattled over the uneven terrain as we progressed through the tunnel of weaving branches and thick pines. In the distance there came a white spot—an opening. We punched through a short wall of snow into a clearing. The tires squelched and the brakes grinded like metal scratching metal as we came to a stop. Up ahead about one hundred yards was a line of trees guarding the entrance to more forest. There was no longer a previously carved out path for the truck to proceed.

"All right," my father said, shoving the column shift into Park. "We walk from here."

Again I thought about his straight-faced joke about leaving me out here.

Just a joke, I told myself.

Just a joke.

Before we left the vicinity of the truck, my father stepped around back and opened the lift gate. Inside the bed was a long black bag similar to one that would hold a guitar, except thinner, and I didn't believe for a second that we'd come out this far just so we could sit down by some makeshift campfire and play Stairway to Heaven.

"Let's go." He slammed the gate shut and we were on our way hiking toward the tree line.

I didn't have the best boots for this excursion. Blue-light specials at K-Mart during the Christmas season. It wasn't long into our trek through the woods that my feet felt double their weight, and sodden as if I'd been trampling through a marsh in thick wooly socks. My father kept a determined pace. I struggled in his shadow. Not that he complained or urged me on, though he did shoot disapproving looks over his shoulder whenever I stepped on a branch that broke or kicked a rock that skipped away, the sounds magnifying and carrying through the barren forest.

It felt like we had walked for hours before reaching the next clearing. Just short of the woods coming to an end, my father stopped dead.

Mildly alarmed, I stopped moving as well. In the dead of winter there was hardly any life to the woods. A few caws from a murder of wayward crows off in the distance, as well as the faint trickle of a nearby stream. By the way he hunched to peer through the trees, I could tell my father saw something out in the open. He gave me a finger-to-the-lips gesture for quiet and then signaled me to come join him.

Like a burglar traipsing through a mesh of red laser wire to get at a diamond, I carefully maneuvered my way through the thicket of severed branches and dried leaves, cautious not to cause any noises that might alert whatever it was my father was looking at and give away our presence.

Together we made our way nice and slow toward the clearing. I was trying to be conscious of where my father stepped, making sure I planted my own steps in accordance. The trickling of water picked up, reverberating off the stillness of the dead woods. My father stopped again, just short of the tree line, and held up a fist. I didn't know many hand signals used in the military, but this one was easy to recognize. I stopped mid-step and held my breath.

My heart sped up watching him continue to creep ahead a few more feet. He was stalking something like a predator would a prey. He crouched down behind the fat, solid trunk of a maple. I remained absolutely still until he beckoned me over, having again pressed his finger to his lips as a reminder.

When I got up beside him he carefully started unzipping the long bag he had lugged over his shoulder from the pickup. The movement of the stream was louder than the teeth of the zipper lining coming apart. He didn't open the bag all the way, but just enough to reach in and take out the rifle that turned out to be about as long as I was tall.

My mind flashed to the black handgun that sat on his nightstand.

With precision and silence, he armed himself. The butt of the rifle nuzzled up against the inside of his shoulder. His eye went right to the scope mounted on top. The business-end of the rifle was directed out to the right.

His eye peering through the scope never once blinked. The muscles of his face didn't flinch, or tighten. No part of his arm or the long weapon shook or wavered. He was a statue. Hardly a wisp of steam exited his nose or mouth whenever he exhaled. Much as I made to mimic him in that moment, I couldn't. I lacked so much of the finesse and control he'd built up to perfection over the course of his military life.

He glanced over to me, not moving away from the scope. "Wanna see something?"

My breath escaped in jagged tendrils of white clouds. I nodded.

He gestured for me to get right up close to him. He lifted the rifle and placed it around me in an awkward embrace with his arm encircling me. I knelt exactly as he, right up against him. I got a whiff of the musk on his skin, and the tangy citrus soap he had used to shave with. It was a familiar smell—only ever his.

"Take it," he said.

I swallowed big in reluctance but had no chance to voice a concern. While he supported most of the weight, and kept his right hand wrapped over the trigger so it wouldn't go off, the length of the weapon's stock was lowered into my hands. I could feel its oppression, the mass of its power, and in that came a deep thrill in knowing I was holding something that had the ability to steal life.

"Tell me what you see."

Peering through the scope, besides the crosshairs and slight measurements of the reticle etched into the glass, there was a clear close up of a tree at the far end of the oval-shaped clearing. I could make out the intricacies of the bark's ridges and crevices almost two hundred yards away.

"Looks like a tree," I whispered.

He started guiding both me and the rifle a few degrees right. The long steady breath through his nose was soothing in my ear. "How about now?"

We were skimming along a narrow stream, the fringes of which were frosted with clean white snow. Then came the flutter of a tail, followed by the speckled hind of an animal bent down to the water.

"Wait," I said. He halted the tracking of the weapon.

As if it heard me, the deer stopped drinking. Its long and slender neck went from being arched like the curve of a rainbow to straight up in alert. The doe's ears flicked upright and twitched. Its tail stood straight out. It stayed that way until the distant crows cawed again, after which it relaxed, the tail fluttered, and the deer went back to lapping at the stream. The coat of the animal was clean, smooth, spotted white with the rest of the body a light brown, its stance elegant.

"Beautiful, isn't it?" my father said, the admiration thick in his tone.

It *was* beautiful. Even at my young age the serenity of what I could see through the scope wasn't lost. Living in the town of Serling Oaks my whole life, wild animal sightings were limited to mangy squirrels chasing each other up trees, opossums digging through the trash, and birds shitting on cars.

What made the encounter with the doe all the more impactful was watching as three fawn emerged from the woods on the opposite side of the clearing and joined her at the water. There was a buck, too, but he remained back at the trees, watching, his antlers filed to such fine points that impalement would be effortless.

Every few moments, while the little ones drank, the mom would turn her head in our direction. Whether they detected us or not, they didn't seem to consider us malevolent. They remained on guard anyway. Suspicious, and rightfully so, considering it was the scope on a rifle that allowed me to watch them.

Which also brought on a chilling sense of prickling dread when reality sunk in.

"We're hunting them, aren't we?"

My father remained mum, but I knew the truth. We hadn't come all this way just to hide out and watch deer going about their routine through a crosshair. This was my test. My father didn't bring me to observe and admire. A pair of binoculars would have done the trick. No, he was looking to bond over a pastime of his.

"You want me to kill one," I said.

The way his face changed told the story.

"No," he said. A lie.

I knew, and he knew that I knew, but we went through with the lie anyway.

Eventually the deer moved off. We watched them go, then started back toward the truck.

"Hot dogs for dinner," my father said.

"I like hot dogs," I said, almost proudly, but not laying it on too thick. As a child, I liked hot dogs a whole lot more than I liked deer.

"So your mom . . . is she . . ." My father stumbled for words. "Is she seeing anyone?"

This came out of the blue just shortly after we got back on the road. He seemed really interested but tried passing it off as a casual inquiry. His eyes darted back and forth between me and the winding lane through the hillside. Given the position of his bare hands on the steering wheel,

I took note once again that he continued to wear the silver band around his third finger. If the years had been unkind to the vows between he and my mother, it didn't reveal itself in the simple ring that caught a casual glimmer off the dull gray light of the day.

"She still wears her ring too," I said.

This seemed enough to satisfy him.

Between seeing my father tear up in mentioning his struggle in the aftermath of shooting a child, and then emote such concern over my mother (though he tried his damnedest to conceal it behind a spontaneous question that, to me, said he'd been thinking about it all along), as well as voice his intentions to reclaim the family he once abandoned, I found that there was something he and I shared in common after all.

Turned out both of us had issues when it came to presenting our true feelings.

When the sun, filtered to dimness through a soupy haze of clouds, began to sink behind the trees and crawl closer toward the westward hills, the temperature inside the house crept lower and lower. I had been in the middle of a round of Sonic 2 (the batteries near dead) when my father called from downstairs.

"Wanna give me a hand in the basement?"

The cellar was divided into two large rooms. The first contained all of the appliances—washer, drier, work sink, woodstove, and water heater. He led me through to the second room, where, stacked to the ceiling against one cement wall running the entire length, was fresh cut cherry wood. In the center of the room was a table saw beneath a pair of fluorescent bulbs. The floor was covered in sawdust.

"Got plenty of wood to feed the stove till spring," he told me. "But gotta make some of the pieces smaller to fit—door's not so wide as I'd like." Then he looked at me, a hint of mischief wrinkling one eyebrow. "You wanna run the saw?"

He knew my mother would never go for this. Even the way he asked suggested we keep this between us, like it was taboo. And though she learned many of the things that went on that weekend, including that which was still to come, I can say with total honesty the silent agreement between my father and me to never disclose the following to her remained an unbroken pact. And currently being six feet under is assurance enough that she'll never read this.

I won't lie, the table saw made me a little nervous, and that was just looking at the teeth of the blade while the machine was still off. When it purred to life, I was initially concerned I had wet my pants. This was beyond any experience I previously had with tools, which maxed out with a Swiss Army knife that my friend Jerry had gotten hold of (likely through his klepto tendencies). But I found, much like the rifle, once the pressure was on to actually use the thing, a rush of exhilaration chased away the hesitance.

My father provided me gloves and goggles and demonstrated where to place my hands on the sides of the cherry wood so that I still had them when the cut was over. The first time, he guided me through. It was both intimidating and thrilling to watch and *feel* the wood being sliced into two with hardly any resistance. There was a tingling in my hands beneath the gloves. The second time he let me do it on my own.

The fresh scent of cherry wood dispersed throughout the room in a spray of sawdust.

My father gathered more pieces to be cut—keeping me busy helming the saw. After enough pieces were made small enough for the stove, he led me over to where he fed the fire. He let me close and latch the heavy steel door. By the time we were upstairs, the decadent cherry heat was wafting out of the vents.

I was setting the table for dinner, the hot dogs had just been set on the grill out on the porch, when my father sat down at the table and asked if I wanted to see a magic trick.

From the breast pocket of his shirt he pulled a quarter. In his other hand was a black permanent marker which he used to fill in a dark circle in the middle of the coin, blacking out Washington's profile as if it was something to be censored. He held out the coin, the side with the black dot facing me.

"First," he said, "I want you to take the coin and inspect it; make sure it's real and that I did nothing to it other than the dot."

I inspected the coin. Seemed genuine to me. Even noted the date etched into it was 1983.

"Okay," he said. "Now I want you to put that quarter into your pocket—any pocket."

I did—the left rear pocket of my Levi's.

"All right. Now I want you to choose the magic words, like Abracadabra, Presto-chango, or ta-da!"

I looked at him strangely. "Who says presto-chango?"

He cracked the knuckles of both hands, then rubbed his palms together vigorously. "For this trick I am going to make the coin vanish from your back pocket and make it reappear back into this pocket." He indicated the breast pocket of his shirt from which the coin came.

I scoffed. Yeah, okay.

He waved his hands around in a grand sense of mumbo jumbo showmanship, spewing all kinds of nonsensical phrases, finally asking me to say the magic words.

I shrugged. "Presto-chango!"

He clapped. His eyes twinkled with a dancing liveliness from the shine of the overhead light. "The coin," he said with a sense of confidence, "is now in my pocket."

My nose wrinkled. "Show me."

He reached into his breast pocket and produced a quarter in the palm of his hand. At the same time a grin stretched across his face. I inspected it closely. The mug of George Washington had indeed been blotted out with black permanent marker, so I checked the date. Sure enough: 1983.

"Bullshit!" I blurted out.

"How do you figure?"

"You had two quarters from the same year," I explained. It was the only logical explanation. "You had one in your pocket with the dot already on it and drew a dot on the second one that you gave me. All you did was take the second quarter out of your pocket—that's not magic!"

My father considered this. His once beaming expression faded. "Huh . . . guess I didn't think this one all the way through."

I grinned, which I think was what he wanted all along.

He excused himself to check on the hot dogs. When he was gone I reached into my back pocket for the original quarter. Except it wasn't there. I only managed to feel up my own butt searching for it. The pocket was completely empty.

"Son of a bitch . . ."

Still don't know how he did it.

I suppose now I can tell you the worst of it.

SUNDAY

The screaming came again that second night.

It was twenty after two when my eyes opened to his howling. Much like the previous night, I tried to muffle the sound with the comforter and pillow pressed to my ears. No dice. Just knowing his cries were happening kept me awake. A vision of him writhing around on his bed haunted me when I tried to close my eyes against the sounds. I also pictured the gun on his nightstand. Remembered the creeping fear of how he sleepwalked down to my room, possibly with the gun in his hand. How he stood over me.

I had to wake him.

Fully wake him.

Once again I peeled myself from the bed and followed the relentless echoes of his cries down the darkened trail of the hall. Once again at his doorway I peeked inside to find him drenched in a cold sweat and flat on his back, twisted among what was left of the bedsheets, his body reacting to an unseen force strangling his mind. His head turned one way, then the other, and back again. He grimaced, but kept his eyes shut. All as before.

I once again made my approach on the left side, where the bedside table and lamp was. Where the black handgun was. And for the briefest of moments, as my hand went for the neck of the lamp, I let my fingers graze over the heavy cold steel. It felt forbidden. I figured after popping on the light I would just nudge him awake as gently as possible. He may not like it, and he might've gotten upset with me, but there was a possibility he didn't even know what the night terrors were doing to him. No one else had been here to tell him.

I found the knob and turned on the light. In response his muscles flexed. His tatted arms, the ribbons of barbed-wire and inked flowers, twisted and turned. His hands clenched under the soft spotlight.

As soon as I placed a gentle hand on his shoulder, he tensed and thrashed, still asleep.

"Dad?" I said, softly. That word still tasted funny, though didn't feel nearly as strange anymore. I was getting used to saying it again. I touched his shoulder once more, offering a little shake. "Dad?"

He moaned, as if in pain.

I shook him again. "Dad." Louder this time.

His face scrunched. Eyes squeezed tighter shut. He gasped.

I became sterner, determined, shaking harder. "Dad."

He cried out, as if I was the one torturing him. I should have known better and stopped there, seeing it wasn't working, but I didn't. In my own agitation, I wasn't thinking about his years of combat training. Back then I had no idea about what PTSD was. I didn't anticipate the response of waking someone who solely depended on his fragile instincts to keep him alive. And for all of this, I paid the price.

"Dad!"

His reddened eyes shot open like they were going to burst right out of their sockets. Already I knew it wasn't him lying there. It wasn't the man who recognized me as his son. It wasn't the man I could reason with. This force about to come at me was the combination of a unique set of combat training skills and the past's haunting choices.

Before I could stumble back a step, he was on me. Quickly I found I couldn't breathe against his bare hands clenched around my throat. It happened so fast.

We were falling. He was looking at me the whole time but not seeing me. He was seeing on my face everything that terrified him, threatened him. Everything he hated.

I reached out for anything to catch me as we fell. I only managed to swipe the lampshade and then grip a leg of the bedside table as it, too, toppled over.

I landed hard, the back of my head smacking off the floorboards. I braced for the falling lamp to nail me in the mouth but it landed next to my head, grazing my left ear.

Any fight I had was immediately extinguished. The weight of him on me, his unleashed strength squeezing out every last bit of life in me, coupled to make sure this wasn't going to be a long struggle as he panted, drooled, and grunted, unaware of what he was about to do.

A glaze settled over my eyes. Things started to dim. This was it. I actually felt it all slipping away as if I was entering a tunnel, sliding backwards, far and away. A strange calm settled over me. The volume began to lower. Colors turned to shades of white and grey. The ache in my chest from the deprivation of air had begun to diminish. My grip on his hands weakened—my own hands releasing and falling lifelessly to the floor at my sides.

That's when I felt the gun.

It had fallen to the floor beside me with the tipped over table. It was out of pure preservation that I was even able to feel around to find the barrel, the trigger, the handle. In a surge of desperation, I regained a smidge of adrenaline, enough to find my grip. There was no time to reconsider, no time for second thoughts. This was my survival.

I was going to have to shoot my father.

I tried blinking away the puffy spots and tears that spread like cataracts over my vision. The weapon was heavy. I didn't know where to aim, and barely had the time left, or the energy, to figure it out. My finger found the trigger. The world darkened. I was out of time, out of air, out of fight, and so, I pulled.

Piercing through the dark that had flooded over my eyes came a brilliant blossom of white and yellow and orange sunlight that filled the room. It was there for a hair of a second then gone. The concussive explosion that immediately followed slammed through my body in a wave of stinging vibration. My arm was thrown back, the gun flung from my weak grasp.

My father's grip released. His body fell to my right, the weight crushing me lifted. The rush of incoming air was intoxicating. The first breath was deep, hurt like hell, and tasted of gunpowder. I coughed, felt woozy, felt like I would throw up, but just kept right on sucking air because that's all my body would do. The only thing keeping me awake was the thought that I had just killed my father.

When I regained some strength all the numbness faded away. Colors returned to my vision, sounds no longer came piped through a tunnel. I grasped my throat and then began sobbing uncontrollably at the sound of my father calling out my name.

He was there. He was hovering over me, asking if I could hear him, asking if I was all right, repeatedly saying how sorry he was. All of this over and over. I hadn't killed him.

I could only croak as the tears spilled down my face. "Dad . . ."

Through gasps and tears of his own, he started thanking God.

When my vision sharpened, I could see the bullet never got him. A small hole had been punched through the plaster ceiling just over my head. My aim had been way off.

Thank God indeed.

It felt like the ringing in my ears lasted the rest of the night. I couldn't sleep, just watched the sun come up large and bright, burning off the gloom. My throat was sore and a bruise formed a ring around my neck. Once we were beyond the fact that each of us was okay—much as we could be, I suppose—my father shut down. He sent me off to my room, where I sat awake and sobbing into the pillow, while he paced about the attic, the hall on the second floor, and then the downstairs. Shortly after the sunrise he came up to my room, whilst a single crow squawked outside the window.

"I just spoke with your mom. She's on her way."

He avoided me the rest of the time. I played my Game Gear until the batteries died.

Mom arrived about an hour later. I heard the Jeep pull in, cutting through a thin blanket of fresh snow in the dirt drive. To her credit, when I went downstairs to meet her in the foyer, she didn't appear or act distraught or angry when she came in the door.

"Hey buddy." I ran into her embrace. She combed through my hair with gloved fingers. When she got a good look at me I could tell she noticed the bruising, but made not a mention or much of a reaction to it. She simply took a breath to steady herself and said, "Got your things?"

"Morning, Maggie."

My father was standing in the entryway to the kitchen, holding open the swinging door. "I just put on some breakfast if you two would like t—"

"I think we're just gonna get going, Scott."

He didn't attempt to argue.

I grabbed my bag.

"Noah," he said. "It was good to see you."

Polite as she could, Mom ushered me out the door.

From the distance we were apart, it looked like tears fell from my father's eyes as the front door closed between us.

We came to a stop at the only red light along Dalton's main road. My mother waited till then to start her questioning.

"We have a long drive back, you know. Are you gonna tell me what happened?"

I swallowed, and it hurt.

"Noah?"

Ahead of us through the light was a sign for the interstate heading north. The entrance ramp was two miles away.

"Noah?"

I know she was fighting her maternal instincts, the protectiveness she had for me, desperately wanting to know what had happened that prompted the weekend cut short, wanting to know how I'd gotten the red and purple marks around my neck, but trying not to push too hard. At the same time my own defenses were breaking down. My throat hurt so much (you never realize how many times you swallow throughout the day until it feels like a shard of glass going down every time). I tried to maintain, tried to hold myself together, and, without thinking of it, touched the base of my throat.

And with it came a terrible vision.

"Noah, please say something."

I flipped down the visor to see myself in the tiny rectangle mirror on the other side. The shape of the bruise almost made a perfect ring.

The light turned green, but my mother had yet to notice.

"What is it?" she asked, watching me study my neck.

I flipped the visor back up. A car behind us blatted their horn. "We have to go back."

Mom asked questions, but I didn't answer them because I didn't know. I didn't know for sure what I would find when we got back to my father's farmhouse. Over the course of the weekend he shared his guilt with me about killing the boy two years ago and the downward spiral that followed from that point, and his new determination to right the wrongs once he was strong enough. And it was all dependent on this weekend with me. I know that was the truth. I was his starting point on the long road to redemption, the long twisted road back in the direction of home. But what happened overnight was a setback from how things were supposed to go.

I flung open the passenger side door (the cover story to my mother was that I'd left my Game Gear behind) before the Jeep stopped completely. She called after me as I bolted for the porch steps. Thankfully the front door wasn't locked.

I called for him the whole way, racing up the stairs. He didn't answer.

At the top of the steps I was hit by a dense, and quite familiar chill that smelled of musty air.

The attic door stood open.

I kept calling for him—louder and louder—hoping he'd heard me and would stop. There was no way to prepare for what I would see after climbing those attic steps, keeping my head down under the slope of the roof. Though I anticipated it, imagination sometimes has nothing on reality.

My father was three feet off the floor, the rope a tight necklace. He was standing on the edge of the worktable. The rope had been run up over a beam among the rafters. He was surrounded by pictures and faux butterflies scattered all over the room.

"Dad . . ."

His eyes blazed, perplexed. "Noah . . ."

I was reduced to a blubbering mess. My throat rasped, words hard to come by. "No . . . Dad . . . don't do it."

I could see calling him Dad meant something. It gave him pause. It was then that I understood, truly, what this weekend had been all about. He'd planned to hang himself long before I had ever been invited to come stay—that was evident by the planning of this shrine. His demand to see me was his reaching out for help. He wanted to be saved.

He wanted *me* to save him.

Calling him Dad proved to me that I could do it.

"It was an accident," I said, touching my neck.

"I could've—" He was crying.

"But you didn't! I'm right here. So that means you have to come down."

I stood my ground in this faceoff. I couldn't afford one second of hesitation as the front of his feet already hung over the edge of the table. That he didn't take those fatal steps meant I was making headway. I had to keep pressing him.

"Please," I said. "You wanted me to save you—let me save you."

"I hurt you. And your mom."

"I forgive you." And when I saw the effect of these words, I came at him with a few better. "I love you."

Now let me explain the power of what I said.

Back then, back in 1995, the words *I love you* meant a whole hell of a lot more than they do today. Right now the word *love* is misused and abused, bestowed far too often in meaningless ways, diminishing its value when spoken with truth. Today we tell our spouses, our family, our children that we love them but in the same breath we proclaim how much we love our iPhones.

Love, back then, spoken by a twelve-year-old boy, was pure, and not tainted by the vices of the adult world.

It was what got him to remove the noose and come down off that table.

We held each other and cried for a long time that morning before my mother came looking for me, calling throughout the house that she'd found my Game Gear in my bag. She was speechless when she came upon us in the attic. She noticed the shrine, the rope, the growing puddle of tears between me and Dad, but she never spoke a word of it. She joined us on the floor, adding her own tears to the pool.

That evening I was back in my house, in my own bed. I remember thinking, after the light was out and the only thing in the world was the breathing wind outside, that after everything that had gone on that weekend, I was so glad there was no school on Monday.

CODA

Before I began this recollection, I wrote these words: *Sometimes there are far greater costs than paying with your life.*

I never truly got over that weekend with my father—part of that is because I believe *he* never got over it.

Guilt clung to his bones over the years, manifesting like a cancer, which is ironic since that was what ended his life just a few short years ago. At the end of his life my father fixated on all his wrong-doings. Many who repent late in life (your God-diggers, as I've come to call them) are the same way. My forgiveness was never enough, except at the most pivotal moment—bringing him down off the ledge.

Mercifully, he's now free.

I hope he found peace before the end. I know that's out of my hands, but never out of my mind. It's kept me up nights, especially in the dead of winter, as I lie next to my wife, listening to her snores and staring into the video screen of the baby monitor at my bedside. My daughter will make a noise, and I wonder, as I watch her roll over to find a new comfy spot, if I'll let her down someday the same way my father did with me.

Will then, I ever be able to forgive myself, as my father never had?

I guess, in time, I've come to understand him more and more.

As I also mentioned previously: this summation of the events was an idea suggested by my therapist. I followed through. Another of her ideas was that I choose a memory of my father that'll influence a better appreciation of the man over time.

I have one, but first let me tell you of my mother.

My parents never got back together. They, instead, found an understanding and formed a low-key relationship that was more for my benefit than theirs, I suppose. I continued living with Mom, and visited Dad occasionally. She never remarried, and I don't think she ever wanted to. She made friends at work, volunteered at soup kitchens, and got out more. I think watching me get older and carve out my own place in the world was enough for her, sadly. If there's one thing to feel blessed over it's that before they each met their passing, Mom and Dad met their granddaughter, Ellie.

Last week was the first day of spring. The thaw is still a way off here in upstate New York, which isn't uncommon. Recently, I took a drive down to Dalton.

I bypassed the town. Didn't bother going by the old farmhouse, but instead followed the winding roads out to the middle of the countryside where there are no paved roads even today. I turned down a rocky trail that cut through the woods and stopped in a clearing. I walked from there. For an hour I trekked before coming to a second clearing.

There I saw a family of deer drinking at a stream.

My hope is that this is the memory of my father that will replace all of the others.

AUTHOR'S NOTES & ACKNOWLEDGMENTS

If you've read my previous two novels—*Seeing* and *The Painted Lady*—you've likely noticed that this one was a bit shorter. There's reason. With this story I challenged myself to do something different, which was focus solely on the relationship of Noah and his father from beginning to end and never straying. This meant keeping to a single stretch of highway without backtracking, diverting for a bite to eat, helping a stranded motorist, or a stop to refuel. In less metaphoric terms: No subplots.

Subplots, for those uninitiated, are the side stories in a novel (sometimes known as the B story). There's nothing wrong with subplots—subplots are life. If you consider your home life with your family your A story, then going to work every day is your B. My goal here was to be compelling and unrelenting by sticking with Noah's greatest conflict for the duration.

I suppose it is up to you if I succeeded.

This story also marks my first real attempt at writing first-person. This form has both its advantages and disadvantages. Suspense, in first-person, is reduced off the bat simply because you know the narrator will survive. Also there's the tendency for an author to ramble on and on when they inhabit the mind of the central character for the entirety. Hopefully I kept you turning pages, anxious at moments in regards to the outcome, and reduced my ramblings to a minimum.

I also—with this story—tried to be funnier.

Again, that one's up to you.

My wife was the first to read a draft and gave me support and assurance that I was on the right path. I don't know what I'd ever do without her.

My friend, and a wonderful artist, Christopher Wright (clwright. com) did the cover art for this one. Amazing job, Chris. Can't wait to see what you come up with next!

Jessica Kristie at Winter Goose has offered countless support and lets me do my thing. This one's already co-dedicated to her, but enough thanks from me could never be overstated.

Special thanks also goes to my fantastic editor, James Koukis. He always gives me the fine-tuned once-over and makes sure I'm ready to go out in public without a missed button or my fly down. James did an exceptional job here.

I always try to work something about my daughter into these end-notes. For those wondering: her birth and the story of Noah's are very similar.

Finally, a big thank you to my readers, old and new. I realize, despite what I wanted to achieve with this tale, I gave you a thinner book this time around, and it'll be a little while before there's a new one from me (gonna take some time away from self-imposed deadlines and stressful writing goals to spend time with my girls), so, what follows is "bonus material" of sorts in the way of a short collection featuring nine additional stories—micro-stories—that I hope you enjoy. Two of them, "The Morning After" and "Answering The Call," were previously published— were actually my first two published pieces of fiction. Two others, "The Lady in the Park" and "At Sundown," are brand new, and just for you. The remaining five are original tales in a series I wrote as lead-ins to my second novel, *The Painted Lady*. And while the "Tales of The Painted Lady" stories can be enjoyed on their own, they work better in the context of that novel. I included them here for those who read that book and would like to revisit some of those characters.

Side note to anyone who reads this and happens to reside in Dalton, Pennsylvania: I've been there a few times, know the layout pretty well, but took some liberties with your town in order to meet the demands of my fiction. What can I say, it comes with the territory.

—J.F. *April 16, 2016*

Tales of The Painted Lady #1
Moving Dad

The last box of her dad's things came out the front door, carried in the arms of the tenant who lived on the first floor of the duplex. Claire could have carried it herself—it wasn't heavy, just the odds and ends: a few paperback books with the spines completely intact, the roll of packing tape used to seal the other boxes, some dishtowels, packages of loose batteries, a pair of scissors, a fork discovered in the back of a drawer—but the man insisted on helping when she first started carting boxes out the front door, said with a smile that he had nothing better to do.

"Thank you so much." Claire accepted the last bit of her father's things and slid it atop the other boxes stacked in the back of her van. She wore a weary smile while sweeping the strings of her blond bangs away from her forehead.

The man waved this off and shrugged, letting her know it was no big deal. "Your dad gonna be okay?" With his bearded chin he made a passive gesture at the front passenger seat where the elderly man named Lou sat, staring blankly out the front glass.

Claire sighed. "Yeah. This will be better for him. And me. Just got to be too much coming here and taking care of things every day. I have a husband who's needy enough and *doesn't* have Alzheimer's."

The man shared in her laugh. It felt good to laugh, even if it came more out of exhaustion and relief than it did pure joy.

"Well," said the man, "I'll sure miss seeing him up on his porch and waving to him every day. Seemed whenever I came out to go for walks your dad was looking out, just keeping watch over the street I guess."

This garnered some interest. Claire asked if her father ever waved back or said anything in return.

"Umm . . . no," said the man after a moment's thought. "I can't say for sure he ever did."

Claire accepted this truth with a heavy heart, but flashed another tired smile to reciprocate. This wasn't surprising news but it was still difficult to hear. Many months after the diagnosis had time to sink in, she accepted her father was no longer the outgoing, independent, and *aware* person he once was. Right before her eyes, like some evil magic trick, he had withered away, his liveliness receding into an invisible shell. It was rare anymore to catch little bursts of his character come out of dwelling so deep within a blank slate. For Claire the struggle had been imagining her father spending the days she couldn't be at the apartment every waking hour as a complete vegetable. Or doing something dangerous.

That's why he was coming to live with her and Eric. Besides it being easier to tend to her father's needs in her own home instead of driving to the apartment every day, he just couldn't be left alone anymore. No telling what would happen. In a best case situation, he would just sit around all day, but that left messes of its own kind for her to later clean up. Her worst fear was wondering if he'd get a sudden burst of inspiration and try using the stove. Or worse, go out for a walk and not come back. Or even worse than that. At least Eric worked from home and could manage the small things, like supervision, during the day while keeping Skype sessions with the home office in Fort Worth.

Claire closed the back door of the van, resigned to her fate. "Thank you again for helping, Mr. Greene. And for trying to give my father some attention. Hopefully it won't be long before someone comes and takes the second floor so you have some company again."

"I'm not worried about it. I'm sure someone will come along." He then extended his hand for hers to shake. "And please," he said, "call me Miles."

Tales of The Painted Lady #2
For Rent

When the touchscreen of her phone lit up from an incoming call at eight fifteen Wednesday evening, Evelyn's leathery brow knitted. She didn't recognize the number, though the area code said it was local, which meant only one thing: someone was calling about a vacancy in one of her rentals.

She took a long drag off the half-spent cigarette piped between her lips and considered whether or not to answer. It was late in the evening, for her anyway (especially when her internal clock still roused her at four every morning despite her being long retired), and she was comfortable lounging out on her back deck, taking in the scent of menthol mixed with the enticing aroma of burning wood wafting her way from down the block. The late November air was chilly but tolerable.

Though she really was in no mood to talk business, Evelyn had been faced with an exodus of many of her tenants as of late. Revenue was down. The price of smokes kept going up, along with everything else necessary to survive. Young people were either moving back home because they claimed they could no longer afford the lifestyle of being out on their own, or they were shacking up with significant others to save on expenses (just not shacking up at one of *her* rentals). These kids claimed they were in love. Evelyn grimaced at that. In love or not it was costing her dollars and making more work for her to fill the vacancies piling up. She answered the call only because she couldn't afford to miss it.

"Hello?" Her throat was raw, her voice a constant rasp.

"Yes, hi, I'm calling about a listing you have for a first floor duplex on Paden Road."

Ah, yes, Evelyn thought. The end of the cigarette glowed bright from a deep inhale. Her lips pursed tight around the ashy tasting cylinder. Paden. That duplex was one of the few properties she had in her arsenal that featured a low turnover. The location was in the middle of a quiet suburb populated by mostly retired folk like herself. The upstairs unit was occupied by an elderly man named Lou who had been there almost a year. Poor man had been stricken with Alzheimer's, one of Evelyn's biggest concerns now as she approached her eighth decade on Earth. A concern far greater than whatever mounds of tar were sticking to her lungs. The downstairs of the Paden duplex had only just gone up after a university student of four years got her diploma and her full ride out of town to the next institution.

"Have you spoken with Jimmy already?" she asked the caller.

"I did try the other number in the listing, but no one picked up."

Evelyn sighed. Typical that her grandson, who was her handyman and filter for most of her prospective tenants, couldn't be bothered to answer. Likely too busy lighting up himself. Except he didn't dabble in the legal stuff.

"Well," she said, "if you'd like to see the apartment, I can arrange sometime tomorrow in the late aftern—"

"I don't need to see it," said the man. "If it's available, I'll take it."

Evelyn snuffed out the last quarter of her smoke, sitting straight up in her wicker porch chair. "You don't want to see the place first?"

"No need," said the caller. "Just let me know what you want in terms of first month and a safety deposit, and whatever else you need. I'll bring you a check tomorrow."

Evelyn didn't know what to say. This was most peculiar. Never before had she heard of someone taking an apartment sight unseen. She cleared her throat, suddenly feeling skeptical and a little irritated. She wanted to huff on another cigarette immediately. "Is this a joke, son? Did Jimmy put you up to this?"

The man on the other end of the line assured her this was no joke.

She didn't know why, but Evelyn believed him. Something in the sincerity of his voice.

"Well then," she said, "rent is eight hundred, deposit is the same, and I require first and last months'."

"I'll make you out a check," said the man.

Evelyn almost laughed, not because she found the situation funny, but rather strangely absurd. "Who is this, by the way? What's your name, son?"

"Oh, I'm sorry," said the man. "My name is Miles."

"Miles," she repeated.

After the call ended, Evelyn sat back in her chair and lit a new smoke. For the longest time she remained under the starry ceiling of the clear night, a trail of smoke rising over her, wondering what would cause a man, relatively young by the sound of his voice (and young compared to her) to settle so quickly on a home, one that would initially set him back twenty-four hundred smackers, that he'd never seen before.

She wondered what he was running away from.

Tales of The Painted Lady #3
Anniversary

The first temperamental thaw to cut a swath across upstate New York came early, revealing the grass had grown mangy and long at Hillside Cemetery. Except at the grave where Miles Greene stood. The swollen mound of dirt that was fresh in October of the previous year had settled. Wiry patches of grass had sprung through the soil at his feet while all around him sporadic piles of snow still blanketed the earth. The morning had dawned grey in the valley, but now peeks of sun were burning through the cloudy canopy.

The stringy, naked limbs of the weeping willow beside Miles hung still. There were no bugs, no other nuisances like cars driving by on the cemetery roads snaking through the hill, and only the distant sound of a maintenance worker running a pressure washer could be heard among the solemn air hanging about the headstones. He had complete privacy and yet didn't know what to say. It often felt absurd, and a bit cliché, to speak aloud at the grave. Yet it also never felt like he was talking to his wife if the words weren't coming out of his mouth.

With the day being one of significance, Miles decided first to set down the pot of blooming white gerbera daisies he had brought, sweeping aside crusty remains of snow and browned, dead leaves from the base of the marble. The flowers would likely be dead by this time tomorrow, but, he supposed, tomorrow didn't matter, in more ways than one.

"I know it's been a while." He swallowed, and shrugged. "I have no excuse."

The distant spray of the pressure washer cut out. Miles looked around to double-check he was still alone.

"Thought I saw you the other day. In the apartment. Even said something to you before I realized . . ."

He scratched at the length of growing beard irritating his neck. It would be nice, he thought, when the new facial hair got beyond the itching stage. On the plus, it had been keeping his face warm against the winter chill.

"I'm . . ." He had a difficult time getting it out. Miles took a deep breath, cleared his stuffy nose, and resigned to the uncomfortable truth. "I'm gonna go see a therapist. Your brother's idea actually. I guess to him it's weird that I keep seeing you everywhere. Maybe I just shouldn't share everything with him. Anyway . . . my first appointment's on Thursday."

His eyes wandered away.

"Not really anything else going on. Just . . . kind of here."

The pressure washer started up again.

"You got something in the mail—a subscription renewal notice for Cosmo. Kind of strange that you still get mail when I go back to the house to grab the bills. I cancelled it, by the way. Your Cosmo."

Miles sighed. His minute attempt at levity did nothing to ease the heavy lump in his throat, in his chest, anchoring his sorrow.

"Can't believe it's been thirteen years since that day in the café. Right about this time I was sitting in the lounge, looking out the front glass, waiting for you." He shoved his freezing hands deep into the pockets of his coat. "And now . . . here we are."

There was not much else to say. He had satisfied the urge, and obligation, to be there. Miles knelt down and, as was part of the ritual, placed his hand on the top of the stone, just above where STEPHANIE JUDITH GREENE had been etched.

"I'll try not to stay away too long this time," he said. "Happy anniversary."

His steps crunched off the frozen ground as he turned and walked away, forcing himself not to look back at the name on the stone, the settled mound of dirt, or at the small pot of white daisies giving company to the lonely grave beneath the lifeless arms of the willow tree.

Tales of The Painted Lady #4
At All Costs

With little effort he strong-armed the cap off the neck of his beer before discovering it wasn't a twist top. Bryan stared at the impression of the ridges of the cap embedded in his palm and realized he was more nervous than he thought. Standing alone in the kitchen, gripping now at the base of the sweaty bottle—hoping he himself wasn't perspiring nearly as much—he drowned what he could of his apprehensions in a long pull and then poured a glass of Riesling from the bottle on the counter next to him. He took a moment to gather himself—adjusting his tie and his sunglasses, going over his strategy one last time, and tilted his head both ways left and right, far enough to crack his neck—before taking both drinks out to the porch that looked over his wooded yard.

In one of the two Adirondack chairs facing the vast tree line was a woman whose years were at least a decade shy of his own. This was a little off-putting because while Megyn was young, she held a great responsibility as the intern to the curator of the Garland Gallery. And Bryan wasn't going to make any deals unless he went through this pup first.

"Thank you," said Megyn, accepting her Riesling.

"No problem," said Bryan, taking his seat next to her. They didn't sit basking in the quiet serenity of their surroundings for long.

Megyn took a modest sip, barely tipping the glass to her lips. "So, what's all of this buttering me up for?"

Bryan drank again, taking more than a modest sip. "What's that?"

She shot him a glare that said he was kidding no one. "At first I wondered if this lunch date was a way of you offering to represent me.

You've seen my work at the gallery. When Liza lets me put it up on her precious walls that is."

He cracked a smirk. It was no secret between them that Liza Machiavelli, curator of the Garland Gallery in downtown Serling Oaks, had an extremely tough outer shell to crack when it came to getting stuff through her establishment's front door. The pickiest of the picky. And she could afford to be so. But usually once you wormed your way inside you found how soft (and accepting) she really was. It just took a lot of boring to get there. Bryan could only recall a few times he ever saw Megyn's work displayed (and she'd been working under Liza for three years), and those days were usually stuck in the middle of the week when attendance, and eyes on the walls, was low.

"Then," Megyn continued, "when you brought out the salted lamb that your wife prepared instead of you cooking burgers on the grill, and decided to wear a suit to your own house, I realized you didn't want something *for* me. You wanted something *from* me."

Bryan sighed. "You're right, Meg. I should have treated you as smart as you are."

She grinned. "You've already greased the entryway, Bry. Now, what do you want?"

There was no other way to go about it. She had him. Bryan dropped the act, along with his shades.

"You've heard of Miles Greene?"

She blinked her eyes a couple of times, registering the name. "He's local, right? Is that the artist whose wife was murdered back in . . . ?" The horror could be seen dawning on her youthful face. "That was your sister, wasn't it?"

He nodded. She gave her condolences.

"Miles is an amazing artist," he said. "But the thing is he hasn't had a show in forever."

"You want him at the Garland."

Bryan quickly picked up that she wasn't asking. "I do."

Megyn took a moment considering this. The wine in the glass in her hand swirled around the inside with smooth turns of her slender wrist. "Didn't he paint movie posters?"

"For some of the highest grossing films worldwide," added Bryan, slipping back into sale mode.

"He's too commercial," said Megyn dismissively, putting her glass down on the wide arm of the Adirondack. "Liza won't go for it. You know her, she likes people to think her featured artists were discovered and groomed by her. Miles is too well known."

"The gallery has a vacancy in July," said Bryan. He didn't want to overplay this hand, keeping his tone casual and light, yet direct. "You said the featured artist had to bow out the other day when we spoke. Would Liza risk having *no one* during the First Friday Art Walk and be closed when all of the other galleries will be open, with fresh work by artists up on their walls? She could have one of the biggest names to come out of our little area of nowhere. That's a guaranteed full house."

Megyn went quiet over this hypothetical.

"Plus, it would mean a lot to me," said Bryan. "Miles . . . he's had it rough. Doesn't even live in his own house anymore because that's where she . . . He would kill me if he knew I was here begging for him. But he needs this. He needs this, Meg."

She sighed, fully aware her good nature was being taken advantage of.

"I need to know it'll all be new stuff," she said. "He can't hang posters in the Garland. Liza will have my head, and my internship."

Bryan made that promise. The show was only a few weeks away and he didn't know if he could keep that promise, but he made it. He had to. "Does he have the spot then?"

Megyn eyed her Riesling. "You're a good agent, Bryan. Miles is lucky to have you as his. Which is why, if you want me to go in to Liza and fight for him . . ." She sipped. "I want you to represent me."

In her piercing eyes and her unwavering tone, he could tell there would be no budging on this. He had used her good nature and now it was he being held over a barrel. Bryan admired her tenacity, how she played the game.

    She extended her hand. He shook it.

Tales of The Painted Lady #5
From Downstairs

She was burning up one minute, freezing the next. Perpetually her skin was slick with a cold sweat. She was comfortable on her right side for a while and then her lower back would cringe and tighten up and she'd have to roll over to look up at the ceiling to gain any sort of comfort. It was only a few breaths before the muscles in her neck, shoulders, all the way down to the backs of her calves would twinge and she'd have to turn onto her left side. An ongoing cycle. She couldn't taste anything, smell anything, and whatever she coughed up had the consistency (and texture) of tapioca.

Awesome.

Fortunately, her husband, thus far, had managed to avoid catching any of it. And it wasn't for a lack of exposure. He'd made more rounds to their bedroom than a nurse in a maternity ward, bringing with him all kinds of fever reducers, expectorants, and food and juice that felt like swallowing glass when she ingested it. All the while, not one sniffle out of him.

Just as well, thought Stephanie. Had her husband come down with whatever flu this was, she wasn't able to reciprocate the care he'd shown her. Not now anyway, and probably not for a while. She hardly had the strength to blow her nose when she needed to, or carry herself to the bathroom to pee. The latter she kept to herself. Her husband had been there with the box of tissues every time, but she didn't want his assistance getting her to the pot.

Poor Miles, she thought. He would do it, though, if she asked. Poor, sweet Miles. He hadn't wanted to leave her for his art panel in Scranton, but she felt terrible enough that he'd been waiting on her that she didn't want him missing this engagement on account of her. She couldn't let him put everything on hold just to be by her side; they'd been together too long for that. It was cute when he did this kind of thing during the short stint that they dated thirteen years ago, when they were just kids, but now that they'd been married for the last twelve it still surprised her that he hadn't changed much in his devotion to stick by her side—in sickness, especially, and in health.

She smiled at the thought that he would stay with her on a sinking ship if the last lifeboat had only one seat. Even if her own demise was imminent, he would not leave her to save himself. That's the kind of man Miles Greene was. Predictable, yes, and perhaps a bit of a cornball (though, she could be too at times—the cheesy, cringe-worthy lifeboat analogy replayed through her head) but he had proved long ago where his loyalty lied. He remained with her, loving as ever, confident of their future together, despite having found out there would be no children.

That's not to say he had been all smiles, but that was nothing to dwell back on. It was long behind them.

She'd found a good spot on her right side, and was about to doze off, when there came the incredible explosion of glass breaking. Against the stiffness in her back and neck, Stephanie sprang upright. The noise came from downstairs.

"Miles?" Her voice was raw, hoarse.

He didn't answer. She heard footsteps coming up the stairs.

"Miles?"

When the bedroom door opened, it wasn't her husband she saw standing there.

The Morning After

First, there was a numbing awareness. Then the hum of the outside air swirled in his ears as it came in brisk through the nearby open window. Then came the wooziness, and it hit hard before he lifted his head, which weighed twice as much as normal, from the sweat-covered pillow.

Then came the throbbing in his temples, spreading swiftly to his brow.

When Stephen peeked his eyes open a beam of morning sun shone right through his skull, engulfing the enormous loft in painful streams of white. A brilliant buzzing in his ears like static, a piercing in his teeth like a drill, and every strand of hair stretched on his face, which wore only a week's worth of stubble.

Then he remembered the tall, pale redhead in the tight dark jeans he met at . . . Was it the Rathskeller? Barnaby's? No. Not there. Jonathan's maybe? One of the bars on the strip. He hadn't been there long; just ordered his first beer when there came a brushing against his side and he turned to see . . . well, what did he see first? The red hair? Her puffy crimson lips? The body? Those striking green eyes . . .

There wasn't much talking. A few drinks between them—though now it felt like more than a few—and soon enough they were stumbling the two blocks back to his place. It wasn't until they arrived at his front stoop that he even got her name, though he'd be damned to remember it now. Fortunately, for the sake of getting laid, she didn't mind late introductions.

After that everything was a blur—a fast paced, rough-riding blur—and he passed out shortly following.

Is she still here?

Despite the pulsing ache from the swelling inside his head sending out waves of queasiness into the pit of his rumbling stomach, he felt he could muster up something for Round Two.

Except the other side of the bed was empty.

He grunted a thick sigh of disappointment as his vision settled and the early daylight lessened in intensity. The clock on his nightstand read quarter after seven in bright red. He thought it quite unusual for the girl to be gone already. It was Sunday and, unless she was a nurse or a dedicated Catholic, there wasn't anywhere for her to be so early. She sure didn't act like a dedicated Catholic. And who knows when she left—he'd been under so deep he didn't hear or feel her get up to make an exit.

He'd also never been so hungover. Usually he had to work hard to feel any sort of surface buzz the next day, but this . . . this felt different.

Did she drug me? Put something in my drink maybe? Have her way with me and I don't even remember it?

Standing up was a challenge to his balance, and to his bladder. With the assistance of gravity, when he straightened up everything rushed south and he got the instant urge. Scrambling toward the bathroom, he nearly tripped over his jeans in the hall and, through the haze of unsteadiness, tackled through the door.

He didn't even make it to the toilet before his eyes went to the large vanity mirror over the sink. Scribbled in stark red lipstick on the glass was her promise: *See you tonight.* And beyond those enticing words, he saw his own reflection. A pale, sickly reflection. Dark circles surrounded his eyes. His lips were white. And there was the blood.

Touching his throat, he flaked off bits of dried red that trailed away from two small punctures only inches apart. Trickles of fresh blood appeared from the holes.

And then, in his horror, he pissed on his feet.

Answering the Call

When Samantha heard the police dispatcher call code 10-43 over the scanner set on a small end table underneath the living room window, she sighed and rubbed her exhausted eyes. This wasn't going to be the night off like she'd hoped. Moments after the call, the cry of numerous sirens filtered up through the open windows of her twelfth story apartment on the east side. Unfortunately, she couldn't respond yet. She was still waiting on the babysitter.

It was so much easier when Sean was still around. But the responsibility of their little girl no longer fell on his shoulders. Not since he quit on them and walked out.

We always come second, was the line he threw at her repeatedly. He always managed to squeeze it—in some form—into a tight crevice of their argument just before she was set to go out on a call, when she felt most vulnerable, most defeated by his lack of support. And no matter how she tried to defend her position, her responsibility—like a doctor always being on call, she'd say—he was ready and quick with a snooty retort.

We're your responsibility, too, Sam, was another favorite line of his.

And he was right. Of course he was. And she knew it. Which made her decision to not go after him the moment he stepped out their door and plead for him to stay, or track him down later (at least for the alimony) all the more difficult. Going after him meant she was wrong to keep her job. And she wasn't. As it turned out both of them were right, but someone had to lose.

The ring on her third finger, the one she rotated with the other digits on her left hand while holding their one-year-old in her other arm, pacing the apartment, waiting for the damned babysitter to knock, told the world she was still married. But Samantha didn't know if that was a lie. Sean never filed. He never came back, either.

If he did file, the matter of custody would come up.

Would he dare spill her secret out of spite?

Wasn't that the grounds for their split?

Would he really label her an unfit bride and mother—disclosing everything in the process—just to get possession of Haleigh? Just to get back at Samantha and expose the only way to hurt her?

Expose her only weakness . . .

The baby was quiet in her arms as Samantha paced. To hopefully stave off a forming headache that made its presence known with a slight throb along the inside curve of her nose, Samantha pressed the heel of her left hand into the soft sinus pocket under her left eye and held it there, all the while wondering if there was any way her child could sense all of the turmoil their family suffered—if that was why she was so quiet, or if it was due to the sudden foulness expanding in the air.

If only, Samantha thought, a grin forming on her face, if only her own problems could pass just as quickly with someone else to clean up the mess. On that note, she hoped the babysitter showed up soon so she could pass off diaper duty.

Tamara never seemed to mind being called out of the blue to watch Haleigh, and was paid well in return, when Samantha could actually get ahold of the teenager. If Tamara, who lived two floors up, was out with her friends, then trying to reach her was a lost cause. There was no sitting at home waiting on spontaneous babysitting gigs, even at the rate of twenty bucks an hour.

Tamara understood the situation, though, and tried to make herself available as often as she could. Samantha knew the sixteen-year-old was smart and would figure things out eventually, so Samantha let her in on everything.

"Come on, Tam," Samantha pleaded in the same rhythm she was bouncing her child in her arm. It never took this long for Tamara to race down the two flights of steps. On the phone, Tamara said she just had to gather her Algebra assignment and would be right down. What was taking her so long?

Samantha had just enough time to wonder if the girl would ever arrive before there was a knock at the door.

"I'm so goddamn sorry," Tamara said as she entered. A thick green Algebra II textbook was stuffed under her right arm with a sheet of loose-leaf sticking out the top like a bookmark. "My crazy fucking parents—I told 'em I gotta come watch Haleigh, and they're all like 'Doesn't she have anyone else she can call?' and 'What's always so urgent with her?' and all that shit. I just told 'em doctors get paged all the time so what's the big fuckin' deal, ya know—"

"It's fine, Tamara." Samantha handed over her child—anything to stop the incessant teenager's vulgar rambling. Tamara was a sweet girl and everything, but since she hit her most recent spurt in age and growth, it seemed every other word out of her mouth raised the eyebrows of anyone listening. Samantha compared the young adult's vulgarity with the alarming regularity akin to someone test-driving a car—cringe-worthy and awkward. "You know," said Samantha, "if my kid gets her first words from you, I know exactly where you live."

Tamara looked confused. "What do you mean?"

The frequency scanner under the window once again burst to life with a blast of static. The dispatcher gave an update to the 10-43 in progress, continuing to request backup.

As uniforms began to call in their arrival times, Samantha's expression went grim. It was time to go to work. She took in one last look of her child, now asleep in the babysitter's arms. It was a heart-wrenching scene that had become all too common anymore.

"It's all right," Tamara said. "You'll be back."

This is what it had come down to.

Entrusting her baby to a teenager.

Entrusting her secret.

With a few swift moves, Samantha removed her sweater and wraparound skirt, revealing underneath an aqua latex fabric with gold stripes down the sides that made her look more like a late night stripper in a racing outfit than her everyday persona as an English teacher.

Tamara admired the new outfit. "Lookin' hot, Blue Phoenix."

Samantha sighed. "God, I fucking hate that name."

Upon her choice of words, just as it looked like Tamara might say something, Samantha gave the babysitter a dirty look that said *Don't even start.*

The Blue Phoenix label was one she learned to live with, impressed upon her by a newspaper editor who published a picture captured by one of his reporters of her leaving the scene of a carjacking she had stopped. Unfortunately, the name stuck with the readers and was printed everywhere.

"Be right back." Samantha lifted the window screen away and a moment later was gone, swooping between buildings and over-crowded city blocks in pursuit of the sirens and flashing lights speeding away.

All the while she kept in mind how these sacrifices would mean a much safer world for her daughter.

The Lady in the Park

Like everyone, Cleveland had secrets.

And like everyone, he felt the nagging itch to discuss those secrets. He wanted—*needed*—someone else to hear them, someone else to know. There was a desire to spill it all, and hear his own voice profess the ugly things he had done. The dark things. They were secrets that crawled around in his brain and made noises that kept him awake at night in the quiet of his bed. Secrets with teeth that bit and gnawed, and visited him on occasion like an angry ghost.

That's where the lady saved him. Kept saving him.

Her attention, and the precious time for a confession, was bought with food, which Cleveland had plenty to spare, unlike the funds for a real therapist.

He noticed her frail form about a week ago while on his daily walk through the park. It was actually she who approached Cleveland first, as beggars often do.

He'd been resting on a worn out bench near the riverbed not long before she came over, the uneaten second half of a tuna-salad sandwich going stale in his hand. Anymore on his afternoon walks he needed frequent stops. Was it the constant guilt weighing him down that caused his low stamina? His overly ripe age of seventy-nine could also be a factor, but he didn't believe so. Despite the breaks, he was still managing a respectable two-mile walk every day. He was just slower now. More tired. Achy.

Had to be what was on his mind.

To his relief, it was through the lady that he found solace. While she devoured his leftovers, Cleveland realized he had an audience and took the opportunity to bare his sorrows.

By the time she finished and was on her way, he had told her about how he had regularly skimmed money from the change jar his elderly parents kept whenever he went for a visit. They had passed years ago, but the guilt lived within him.

It wasn't a vast sin in comparison to the others, but still one that bothered Cleveland very much. Getting it off his chest was more than worth the price of the half sandwich it cost him, and far less intrusive than a real therapist would be.

The lady didn't question him, didn't judge him. Didn't scrutinize him or proclaim he suffered from mental illness. She also didn't dole out anti-depressants or attempt to give advice. She was just thankful for the meal.

And he became thankful for her.

She was there again that day as he made his approach to the bench, waiting for him. In a bag he carried half of an egg salad sandwich he'd made. The bickering nerves he'd dealt with, cradled in the lining of his stomach, allowed him to intake only a fraction of the meals he prepared anymore. She gladly accepted the rest—and looked like she needed it—gorging herself on most of what he handed out whilst he made his admissions.

"I ever tell you 'bout my son?"

The lady eyed him, but for merely a second before she became fixated on the egg salad he was also busy removing from the bag and unwrapping. The Saran Wrap peeled off easy, the stretching of the clear elastic tantalized her. He knew he could've said anything then and she would go nowhere. Her opening mouth sensed that this portion of egg salad would soon belong to her, and soon wasn't soon enough. But she remained patient. She needed this meal.

As it was, he was about to share the worst of his offenses, and so he held on to the half sandwich just a little bit longer.

"Haven't seen him in . . . six years? Seven?" Then, to himself, "Lord, has it been that long?" He paused to contemplate this. "Not since he brought Sam home to meet us."

Not once did she attempt to break their unspoken pact, even as a hunk of yellow egg salad, once held between the presses of whole wheat bread, dropped down to the dirt at his feet. Her eyes grew. She went to make a sudden move but restrained herself, waiting on his cue.

"My son had girlfriends all through high school. One semester away at Arkham Culinary and . . ." Cleveland shook his head and rubbed the swollen flesh beneath his eyes with his free hand. The guilt that stole his appetite daily rose to flush in his face like a blossoming tulip. He'd told her some terrible things before—like when he slipped his mother's wedding band into his suit pocket instead of on her finger at the end of the funeral like he promised he would.

At that time, almost a year ago now, his sisters had been concerned about any of Mom's expensive jewelry being on her while the coffin remained unattended at the funeral home. Just something about the funeral director they didn't trust. Cleveland assured them he would take care of it, offering to keep their mother's most expensive pieces on him until the end of the services.

But, when the time came, standing at the side of the coffin, alone, just before it lowered into the hole and was forever covered with the pile of nearby earth, he got hit with a disgusting notion.

The thought came after he opened the coffin's lid. After he'd placed upon his deceased mother her earrings, her necklaces, and her golden bangle.

It came when he held her wedding ring—her most valuable piece.

The longer he held it, the longer he discovered he couldn't part with it. Cleveland couldn't bring himself to slip the sixty-two-year-old ring over his mother's cold, limp finger.

He wished the diamond-studded band held more sentimental value than it did—fact was he hated his father so their marriage ending with his passing long ago bothered him very little—because if he looked at it with more heart than he did guessing its monetary value then he might not have gotten struck by the whim to pawn it.

But bills needed paying, and as it happened his mother had nothing of her own to pass on to him but even more debt.

Of course the pawnshop downtown would only go as high as half the value of the ring because, hey, they needed to make something off this deal, too, you know. If they could even resell it, that is. You understand completely, was what Cleveland was told.

It made him sick, but yes, Cleveland said he understood.

In the end, a short reprieve from struggling through bill due dates was what Cleveland was awarded. And a hell of a lot of cramps knowing someone out there, somewhere, was wearing his mother's wedding ring while she lay six feet below. Rest her soul.

He couldn't tell anyone what he'd done. His sisters would've disowned him for the betrayal. His wife, before she too fell asleep in the arms of the Lord eight months ago, would've been beyond horrified. And who would've blamed any of them? Every time he paid a bill with that cash he stowed away, he felt an ugly stab of pain down in the pit of his bowels.

But the lady in the park—he could tell her. He could tell her about everything. And he did.

And she listened, to all of it.

She was the only one he told about his son.

"It's not that I hate him or even his kind. But knowing I'd never be a grandfather—a real grandfather . . . Knowing things would just be different . . ."

The lady blinked.

Cleveland pressed the side of a fist to his lips in order to silence the emotions welling up along with the words recounting his latest confession.

"I know I should just call him . . . but I can't. I can't make myself pick up that phone." And then, "You think he'd even answer if he knew it was me?"

Again the lady blinked. There was no answer from her. She didn't care. He knew that. There was only one thing she cared about.

"I know, I know. You been patient long enough." He ripped off a hunk of the egg salad, getting a good mix of both the bread and the yellowy insides, and tossed it down to the crow.

"You're always good to me," Cleveland said with fondness. "Always an ear."

She hopped closer to the slab of egg salad and pecked at it over and over, seemingly ignoring him, taking in as much as she could and leaving the tattered remains behind for others to scavenge or just to spoil in the grass. After a few hops away from the bench, she propelled skyward, her dark wings extending for flight.

But she didn't travel far.

Cleveland watched the crow take a branch in the claws of her feet overhead. The large maple standing guard over the bench in the park was where she'd made her home. And up there she wasn't alone.

Squinting through elderly eyes, he could barely make out her young, but he could hear them tweeting and screeching for her. They anxiously awaited their meal.

"See you tomorrow," said Cleveland after a grunt as he stood from the bench. "Hope you enjoy bologna and ketchup. Got plenty of that at home."

He also had plenty of confessions to keep her babies fed for a while.

At Sundown

Herb stepped outside with a young man's bounce in his step and looked over the empty lot of the gas station with a measure of disapproval, thinking: *Christ. What a mess.*

Having just closed and the sign turned off, the crumpled candy bar wrappers, snuffed out cigarette butts, and chewed up wads of gum stuck to the oil-spotted pavement was all that remained of the day's hundreds of visitors to the Northside Quick-Fill.

As was routine at the end of the day, logged out one item at a time on the turndown checklist Herb carried with him on his trusty clipboard, he started by wiping the accumulated muck and dead bugs off the pumps and the hoses. Once that was finished, he decided to skip down a few tasks and went for his shop broom in the back of the convenience store to take care of the soiled lot.

He was almost inside, had just cracked open the front door, when something fell, clattering to the floor in the back storage room. The bottom of Herb's work boots scraped the paved stoop as he halted in the threshold. Nothing back there should have fallen—he'd secured all the tools to a pegboard himself. He'd also closed the storage room door before stepping outside. That door was now standing open.

Herb looked up to see the string connected to a bell on the top of the front door was nearly all the way taut; a few more centimeters and the string would've moved the bell, signaling a customer's arrival. Carefully he slid a hand up and pinched the bell's clapper to keep it from making contact. The underarms of his work shirt had gone damp.

Once he squeezed himself through—promising to cut back on the leftover doughnuts from now on—Herb reached for the first blunt object closest to him. Unfortunately, all there was to arm himself with was a bin of discounted umbrellas marked TWO'FER ONE.

There was only a single umbrella with a curved metal hilt. He held it by the opposite end to get the maximum damage if it became necessary to start swinging.

With his weapon of choice, Herb tiptoed across the dirty tiled floor and peeked into the storage room.

Inside was a man. Standing at the sink, the stranger was facing the back wall, both hands under the running water from the faucet.

For Herb there were two options to consider: go in shouting and swinging to scare the intruder out, or go to the counter and trip the silent alarm. Problem with the alarm was that in the dead summer air the cry of approaching sirens would alert the intruder long before the cops pulled into the lot. The man would likely get away if Herb didn't stop him.

So it was option one then.

The dripping, beaded sweat stung his eyes. Herb licked at a dribble rolling over his top lip and tasted salt as his hands wrung over the nylon end of the umbrella. All hesitation had to be cast aside. If this stranger saw fear, or even sensed a little intimidation, he'd have the advantage over Herb, and that couldn't happen.

Before he knew exactly what he was doing, Herb charged into the storage room with the umbrella raised. The curved metal handle lopped over the nearest workbench, cascading screws and nails into the air to fall like hail. He screamed and shouted in a scary rage that he wouldn't allow himself to diffuse until the intruder was long gone.

But the intruder didn't retreat; he hardly looked concerned at all in response to Herb's noisy and anger-fueled entrance into the room. What the stranger did do was sidestep a shot from the umbrella and maneuver a quick takedown that put Herb flat on his back on the linoleum.

Except the storage room didn't have linoleum floors. It was supposed to be smoothed pavement.

"Hey! Hey!" the stranger shouted. Herb struggled, and coughed—

the wind taken from him. "Hey! Listen to me!"

But Herb kept trying to fight. "Get outta here! Go!" He gasped for air. "I'll . . . I'll kill ya. Ya hear me—I'll kill ya." He was weakening, and fast. He now regretted not tripping the alarm instead.

The stranger pleaded, trying to maintain the restraint, "Herb, you have to calm down!"

At this Herb's fight completely deflated. Reduced to a sweaty mess on the floor, he was winded and drooling, his chest heaving. The stranger had said his name. "Who . . . Who are you? How do you know me?"

"My name is Doctor Luden—Gabriel Luden. You know me, Herb. I've been a friend of the family for a long time." Then, after a pause: "I delivered your son."

Herb could barely open his eyes through the pooling sweat to look up at this man, this Gabriel. He sensed a blinding light from the ceiling that couldn't have been in the storage room because the double fluorescent bulbs that hung over the center of the room weren't this bright.

He was able to gasp in one breath, "I don't have a son . . ."

"Yes you do. Think, Herb. He's thirty-four, works as an art teacher. You named him after your father."

Then, Herb remembered. "Jacob . . ."

"You were cycling again, Herb," said this Gabriel. "It's gotten worse the last few nights."

Herb felt the man release him and help him to sit up. This Gabriel then used a dry dish towel to wipe off the sweat. Upon looking around, Herb realized he wasn't where he thought. "What . . . ? The gas station . . ."

"You're not at a gas station, Herb. You're at home."

It wasn't sweat tracing down Herb's face now, but tears. "What?"

"When you were in your twenties you worked at a gas station. As your dementia has progressed, you keep finding yourself there." Gabriel allowed a moment to let this sink in before landing another crushing blow of news: "You're not the young man who worked at the gas station, Herb. You're eighty-seven."

The weight of this revelation not only stole every bit of precious air from Herb's lungs, but sent his mind spinning, grappling with the truth, desperate to recalibrate.

"We're in your kitchen," said Gabriel. Herb looked around to find the table, the chairs pushed in, the fridge, the ceiling light fixture with the hundred watt bulbs. By his side on the floor was a walking cane, the handle of it curved like the umbrella he thought he was holding.

Gabriel said, "I was doing the dishes when you came in. The other night you attacked your son in here because you thought he was breaking into the gas station. He needed some stitches but he managed to get you down before you did any serious damage."

Hearing this brought on more tears, and more of the shaky confusion that was reality piecing itself back together like a combination of different jigsaw puzzles. "But . . ." Herb mumbled. His face fell into his hands as he wept. "It was so real . . ."

"I assure you, it's not," said Gabriel. "To be honest: this is the third time you and I have had this conversation."

Herb could find no response other than to sob.

"I thought exposure to the truth would help, but with this and what happened to your son, I'm afraid we're going to have to go through with the transfer to Windsor Assisted Living. It'll be better for you and safer for your family."

His son. The horrific thought of what he'd done to his son—and having no recollection of it—sent Herb into a downward spiral of emotions where he could only mumble his boy's name over and over as he sat, trembling, on the cold kitchen floor.

"Jacob . . ."

The next afternoon, Herb was placed in his new living quarters at the Windsor Care Assisted Living Center. His family and doctor stayed with him for most of the day as he acclimated. After they left in the evening and Herb had time to adjust alone to his new surroundings—a single furnished living space that was more a lush studio apartment than a barren motel room—he tweaked the blinds on the window, casting away the blinding rays of sun as it dipped below the horizon, and sat down on the stiff sofa.

He closed his eyes and put his head in his hands. He took a few breaths to steady himself.

When he opened his eyes and stood up again, he looked around. There was work to be done.

Christ, he thought. *What a mess.*

He grabbed his trusty clipboard with the turndown checklist, pulled a shop rag from his back pocket, and went to clean off the pumps.

Publication note: The stories "The Morning After" and "Answering The Call" were originally published in RiverLit Magazine (#10 and #12, respectively), 2013 – 2014.

ABOUT THE AUTHOR

As an author of adult and young-adult fiction, Joseph Falank has had many of his stories featured in magazines and online publications. Since 2002 he has worked with children, young adults, and special needs kids in a classroom setting from pre-K through grade twelve. Joseph lives with his wife and daughter in upstate New York.